For all the world he held himsel
He talked big. He made himself
big. Truth be told he was only 5 fc
of the scrawled calculations on the
He boasted from an early age that he was afraid of nothing. It was important that he was afraid of nothing. He was going to be fearless, a hero, even if it killed him. His mother had dressed him as a girl and called him Sweetie, damn her anyway, and he was going to go to some impressive lengths to erase that. He advertised himself as fearless, and said that fear was only for the weak, when he knew, knew well and true and for a long time, that fear was merely wisdom in the face of danger. He ran with bulls and would have run with rhinos if it could have been arranged. But small dendrite cracks were appearing in his world class self-confidence. He wasn't as magnificent, wasn't as expert or unerring. He had started to forget. He cursed the concussions. The white coats had told him he might get better. He did not. They had told his father that as well and Hadley's father, and they did not. He had always filled more space than was in the room. At his times of weakness, and they were growing, when the pain would worsen, his organs, his head, his back, the burns, the black ass days—when they were at their worst—he would try to look and sound immortal. He would try to reconstitute his invincibility. He would try to be more imposing, more celebrated, more mythical. But he knew he was shorter than advertised and that his legendary strength was on the wane, like the moon, after being full for so long, decreases in size and brilliance.

ISBN 978-1-949914-48-1

For information address Crossroad Press at 141 Brayden Dr., Hertford, NC 27944
www.crossroadpress.com

First Edition

THE PARIS BOOK

A NOVEL ABOUT HEMINGWAY'S LAST BOOK

BY ROBERT RISCH

Nothing was impossible—everything was just beginning.

F. Scott Fitzgerald

If you are lucky enough to have lived in Paris as a young man, then wherever you go for the rest of your life, it stays with you, for Paris is a moveable feast.

Ernest Hemingway

We are all broken, that's how the light gets in.

Ernest Hemingway

All stories, if continued far enough, end in death, and he is no true storyteller who would keep that from you.

Ernest Hemingway

PROLOGUE

THE MOVEABLE MANUSCRIPT

The Paris book, the notes for which were released from the custom-made, dusty, cloth-covered trunks which had survived World War II, and spent 30 years entombed in a basement storage room in the Ritz Hotel, would begin a three-year literary odyssey before settling on Max Perkins' former desk at Scribner's. Ernest's publisher and good friend who had been introduced by Scott Fitzgerald and who had fought with others at the firm to get *The Sun Also Rises* published in 1926, and had put into print many other expats, had died of pneumonia in 1947.

Max had told his protégées, that if they were not discouraged about their writing on a regular basis, that they might not be trying hard enough; and when Ernest was besieged by any one of a host of setbacks, Max told him that every good thing that comes is accompanied by trouble. He had also told him that he would have to throw himself away when he wrote, a notion Ernest did not accept. Throwing yourself away, he thought at that time, was not a good idea.

From the Paris Ritz, the moveable manuscript, a dozen or so blue and yellow notebooks mostly hand-written in pencil, and many pages of typewritten stories and sketches, would travel to Cuba, Idaho and Spain before being completed in Cuba in the spring of 1960. During this three-year period, from 1957-1960, Hemingway's physical and mental health were not good. An adventurous life had left him with a diseased body full of serious injuries and the unintended consequences of controversial mental treatments of the day had taken their toll. The mine field leading to his death had been planted long ago and would finally explode on July 2, 1961 in his home overlooking the Big Wood River on the outskirts of Ketchum, Idaho. A. E. Hotchner was a friend and traveling companion of Hemingway between 1948 and 1961. He would go on to write a book about the experience. Hemingway would eventually entrust Hotchner with transporting, from Cuba to New York in 1960, the Paris book manuscript which was published four years later. He is also credited with supplying the title to Ernest's widow.

This removable manuscript took three years to complete and covers, with 20 written sketches, five years of the author's life in Paris from 1921-26. It was a fascinating time. The arts, in a way, were being created in the City of Light—so many movements sprang up, so many new techniques invented. The Paris book would not have come to fruition without the discovery of the notebook-bearing trunks and the incredible cast of expat characters assembled in Paris at that time, each of whom, according to the author, would have a little piece of Paris go with them wherever they traveled.

THE RITZ

He had been in bed, basically from late 1955 to early 1956. Not much of him was in good shape and the prognosis was not all that wonderful. Back-to-back plane crashes in Africa two years prior had left him wounded. The first was a Christmas gift to Mary for a sightseeing flight in the Congo, which left him concussed and Mary with broken ribs. The next morning they boarded another plane for Entebbe where needed medical attention was available. But they were cursed. An explosion ended this flight before it took off. He was badly burned and dangerously concussed yet again. And if all that wasn't enough torture, on an ill-advised fishing expedition two months later, a brush fire broke out and he suffered serious burns. All in all he had two broken discs, a dislocated shoulder, a cracked skull and a ruptured kidney, spleen and liver. He was in pain and difficult to please and he drank more than usual. In October 1956 he traveled to Spain and fell ill with another bout of hypertension and liver disease. Given his propensity to drink, his liver was in for a siege. But in November 1956, things would look up.

Charles Ritz, was one of the few people who knew more about fishing than Hemingway. In 1959 he would write a definitive work, *A Fly Fisher's Life,* somewhat echoed by Ernest's son Jack's autobiography, *Misadventures of a Fly Fisherman: My Life With and Without Papa* in 1976. Ritz had come to America in 1916 and joined the army. After the war he spent years becoming an expert fly fisherman out west. His father died when he was 27. He returned to France in the '30s inventing a fly rod and founding the Fario Club, an exclusive fishing fraternity. He then spent several years helping his mother manage the Ritz before becoming its president in 1953 upon her death.

Charlie had met Ernest at the hotel's entrance as he pulled up in a cream colored Lancia Flaminia. He handed the author a package of royalty payments from his French publisher. "It's really good to be back," Ernest said to his hotelier host, sitting in the opulence of Charley's office beneath the mansard roof atop four stories of luxury.

"Shall I have Frank or Bertin make you a "rainbow"?" Charley asked with a smile.

"Wouldn't the guardians of my liver faint at that list of ingredients… what… anisette, mint, yellow and green chartreuse, cognac and what else… there was something else?"

"Cherry brandy and kummel," Charley added.

Charley and Ernest and AE Hotchner, who traveled with him extensively and would write the author's biography in 1966, spent the better part of an hour considering whiskey, literature and art.

"Brecht died in Berlin and Mencken died in Baltimore," Ernest noted, "he was one opinionated son of a bitch, but he edited the *Smart Set* and the *Mercury* and published Sinclair Lewis and Ted Dreiser. My favorite quote of his was one on Puritanism… he said it was the haunting fear that someone, somewhere, may be happy."

A.E. added that Jackson Pollock had died, having been killed two months earlier in a car crash at the sad age of 44.

"We let Grace Kelly get away," from Ernest, referring to her marriage in Monaco, "a fairytale if ever there was one… and while we're on beauty, Marilyn Monroe just married a writer! For God's sake Charley tell me I'm better looking than Arthur bloody Miller."

There was a slight knock, the door opened and René, a head waiter, entered, smiled, left menus and promised to return soon to take their order. Ernest looked at the menu, smiling and admiring the cream vellum paper.

"In the '20s", he said with a grin, "We ate and drank well and cheaply but that will not happen today, I see." First, he and the others had champagne and oysters—a longtime favorite. Then, as if not to outdo each other, they all had steak *marchand de vin* with sautéed asparagus—all served with a choice of some of Charley's best wines. Then several triple cream cheeses and finally the strong *café noisette* with a small crowd of profiteroles and, once that all had settled, some of Charley's own cognac. It was a good lunch. A Paris-Ritz lunch, better for Ernest's disposition than his health.

"I want to show you the new bar," Charley beamed, "the L'Espadon which should have a special meaning for you Ernest since I can remember you saying 'look at so and so, he drinks like a thirsty swordfish'. But first I have a surprise. Remember the trunks you left when you were first here?"

"Trunks?" Ernest frowned.

"Yes… yes… the ones that have been stored in the cellar for ages."

"I know I've had my head bounced around… but I honest to God don't remember any trunks."

"We think it was March of 1928, there is a small card with that date."

Charley had the trunks, cloth-covered and smelling of must and stale air, brought up to his office. What had arrived was Christmas in November in Paris. The tops were opened and there they were, the treasure trove, his notebooks from Paris in the '20s, in situ, beneath the florid memorabilia of Paris nightlife, the myriad letters, an old shirt, a pair of very worn sandals, a few fishing flies and some racing forms. All in the writer's distinctive hand, trenchant descriptions of the who, when and where of the expat days written in lined schoolboy notebooks and an assortment of wine stained typed notes and partial manuscripts.

"Finally," Hemingway breathed. It was as if the missing suitcase from Hadley's ill-fated train ride from Paris to Geneva had reappeared. "The lost Dutchman has been found," he smiled but then grew serious as he engaged Charley eye to eye. "This is the best gift anyone could have given me… and it couldn't have come at a better time."

He adjusted his glasses and thumbed through several of the notebooks. There was no doubt his writing had diminished. The words were coming much harder now. He didn't call it writer's block but that's what it was. His, however, had a peculiar pathology all its own. Even his old trick of quitting for the day when he was onto something, so that he could take off at top speed in the morning, bore no fruit. But here, here was great material, ready-made for success. He lit up. "It's like reading old postcards to myself," he said in a tone more reverential than expected, even by him. As he read, he spouted names and nouns like a kinder, gentler version of Tourette's. "The Lilas… Hadley... Sylvia…Dos… Scott and Zelda… Joyce and Ezra… good old Evan… Gertrude and Alice… génération perdu… the Seine, forever the Seine…Pascin… Oh my sweet Lord it goes on forever. Thank God it goes on forever. Charley, there could have been no better dessert…félicitations à vous on the profiteroles and your cognac—but nothing could top this."

Inside for a short time he felt young again. *"Merci, merci pour toujours,"* he said sincerely, holding up a notebook. He had been 29 in 1926 when these notes were consigned to the storage room adjacent to the Ritz wine cellars. He had been married to Hadley for five years then and Bumby had been part of the household for three. Those were the best of times, he remembered with sadness. I should've been able to see that. Of all those I've loved and who have loved me… she was the best… God bless her. But any regrets were dispersed into the Paris afternoon by the unbridled happiness at rediscovering the forsaken trunks. Here it was, a memoir of youth, poverty and happiness. He had been relatively without means then, living on his Toronto Star salary and Hadley's trust fund. Their first apartment was very small, he remembered, and for quiet he had rented a room around the corner to write. Then there was the move to Canada and back to Paris with Bumby in tow. Charley's voice broke the reverie. With his endearing smile he noted, "In the Hemingway/Ritz timeline this ranks with your liberation of the hotel in the summer of '44".

A smile widened Ernest's face… then wider still. "One of my best days ever," he remembered. "We reconnoitered in Rambouillet… what… 25, 30 miles northeast?"

"Southwest," from Charley.

"Yes… southwest. It was sort of our own little army with

David Bruce, a colonel's colonel. Morale was high. We were ready to liberate the Ritz. I remember it was a Friday—a perfect day for a drink... but then aren't they all."

In reality the "Ritz liberation march" had been nothing more than a pub crawl. Ernest's jeep and his "army" stopped along the way for drinks... The Travelers Club, the Café de la Paix and, finally, the Place Vendome and the ultimate goal... The Ritz. Champagne, hidden from the Nazis, was fetched and dispatched. If you couldn't toast this, what could you toast?

"Claude Auzello was there to greet you, yes?" Charley asked.

"Yes, he was the manager then and we knew each other well."

"I remember hearing that Mr. Fitzgerald had introduced you to our hotel."

"Yes, it was Scott," he said, a certain sadness occupied his senescent eyes. "Back then I had only enough francs to drink here one day a week. Scott had more."

"But you made up for it in 1944."

"Indeed, we made up for a lot that summer."

In the afternoon of Friday, August 25, 1944, under orders from Eisenhower, General Jacques Leclerc and his second French armored division along with several American units entered Paris. There were still pockets of German resistance but the City of Light was finally free from the Cimmerian shade of German control. Hemingway had been seen by some as a faux cannon in the liberation of Paris—or at least of the Ritz—or at least of the Ritz bar. Maybe a cannon, but a loose one.

Ernest stood and walked slowly to a window. "I love this place. There is so much of me here, more than I thought and it is not just because you have such a stunning bar... and I just might qualify as an established expert on the subject. My bar credentials are, unfortunately, unblemished—aside from this first class place, I've studied too long and too often taken refuge at Harry's in Venice, Chicote's in Madrid, Sloppy Joe's in Key West and the El Floridita in Havana. All great, all aces, but not like Cesar's son's place." He turned from the window and held out his hand to Charley who took it and held it in his own for longer than either one would've guessed. "Thank you Charley."

He stood there even after he dropped Charley's thin, strong, fly fisherman's hand. Part of him wanted to ask these two friends some truth or dare questions but that piece of conversation did not fit the available space left in the afternoon. There were answers he wanted to hear. It was 1956 and he had just been given a memoir from 30 years ago. He was retracing the steps of his youth but knew he was entering the stadium for the last lap. He knew he was failing... both body and mind. But he had questions, questions which heretofore he had no interest in considering, but now he wanted to hear answers... at least he thought he did. Am I a bully? Am I a braggart? A boor? A bigot? Would some answer yes to these? Would everyone answer yes to them? As he stood there contemplating these unasked questions, that tormenting thought reoccurred... I was a better writer than I was a man. It was a lethal indictment.

He had spent his life killing things. He was a champion of blood sports and he had the pedigree. His father killed himself as had Hadley's father. He hit people in the nose, apologized, and did it again. He killed all manner of animals, fish and fowl but he wrote harmless, direct sentences. He was a complicated mess of a man who wrote simple, short sentences on which he prided himself, and the literary world built a genre. But once , and he must have been smiling when he did it, in *The Green Hills of Africa,* he pulled a James Joyce—reached into *Ulysses*—took Leopold Bloom by the hand and wrote a 424 word sentence.

For all the world he held himself out to be big. He acted big. He talked big. He made himself look big. He lied about being big. Truth be told he was only 5 foot 11, if you could trust one of the scrawled calculations on the bathroom wall at the Finca. He boasted from an early age that he was afraid of nothing. It was important that he was afraid of nothing. He was going to be fearless, a hero, even if it killed him. His mother had dressed him as a girl and called him Sweetie, damn her anyway, and he was going to go to some impressive lengths to erase that. He advertised himself as fearless, and said that fear was only for the weak, when he knew, knew well and true and for a long time, that fear was merely wisdom in the face of danger. He ran with bulls and would have run with rhinos if it could have been arranged. But small dendrite cracks were appearing in his world class self-confidence. He wasn't as magnificent, wasn't as expert or unerring. He had started to forget. He cursed the concussions. The white coats had told him he might get better. He did not. They had told his father that as well and Hadley's father, and they did not. He had always filled more space than was in the room. At his times of weakness, and they were growing, when the pain would worsen, his organs, his head, his back, the burns, the black ass days—when they were at their worst—he would try to look and sound immortal. He would try to reconstitute his invincibility. He would try to be more imposing, more celebrated, more mythical. But he knew he was shorter than advertised and that his legendary strength was on the wane, like the moon, after being full for so long, decreases in size and brilliance.

"This hotel was Paris," Ernest continued. "It touched everyone I knew here. The Ritz, the rich, it was all the same to me. Fitz had written *The Rich Boy*, which he was becoming, in which he said, 'let me tell you about the rich. They are different from you and me.' We got into a fix over that one I can tell you." A. E. nodded in agreement. "I felt Scott's short story about the diamond big as the Ritz was not his best. The best thing about it may have been the title."

Scott had written a short story called *The Diamond as Big as the Ritz* where Percy Washington boasts that his father is by far the richest man in the world and has a diamond bigger than the Ritz Hotel. On his property in Montana is a mountain made of one solid diamond. But after some rather fanciful machinations the mountain is blown up, leaving the protagonist penniless. For two men who made a production out of eschewing the notion of being rich, both Ernest and Scott seemed obsessed by it. When they had wealth, and they did so more or less at different times, they both said it meant little. However, when they were without it, their need for it was obsessive and dictated a profusion of questionable decisions.

"Were you and Mr. Fitzgerald together often?" asked Charley.

"To misquote Scott, 'quarrels among friends are bitter things. There are no rules. They are not like war wounds—they are more like splits in the skin that won't heal because there's not enough material to mend it.'" Both A.E. and Charley let that hang in the air. Ernest continued, "Scott had money. He was good with it. He lent it to me, sometimes gave it to me, and I think I did not like him for that. He introduced me to Max Perkins, maybe my best friend ever (he nodded to present company as if to exclude them from the calculation). Again I was not appropriately thankful. Then, as happens to men, I rose to his fall. Then I had money and he had none, but rather piles of debts what with Zelda's hospital care and Scotty's tuition and the medicines and rents and God knows what else. The contrapuntal beat of debit and credit. He said it in *Tender...'* The victor belongs to the spoils'... and if we're lucky we can live up to... `Forgotten is forgiven.'" What he didn't say was that he hadn't come to Scott's aid.

Ernest felt a small surprise that Scott's quotes lay so close to the surface of his memory. He went on. "But for him to say that riches never satisfied him, unless they were teamed with charm or distinction... well that was just not true. It was in *Tender* and he started writing that in 1925 when he had money. Unfortunately I've come to know it's a truism that nothing is as obnoxious as other people's luck." Ernest stood quiet at the window and stared at what he wanted to believe to be a cloudless sky but even his myopic eyes could make out a smoky haze, a dimness. There they were, maybe just forming on the horizon, but present none the less... those insouciant puffs on the outskirts of Paris, beyond his apartment above the lumber mill at 113 rue Notre-Dame-des-Champs, beyond the Tuileries, the Café Lilas, the Seine and the rest. It was that gathering darkness that reminded him of the uncomfortable and haunting black ass corners in him, corners filled with shadows that sunlight was having more and more trouble reaching. The very same shadows he had written *A Clean and Well-Lighted Place* to dispel... the troublesome, stinging, tormenting shadows that kept gripping him like the ceiba roots at the Finca. Shadows he couldn't shoot or box or curse away. They were indelible like the forehead scar he'd picked up a long distance in time but not a long distance in space from where he now stood. It was like church for a moment.

"Only one other bar mattered as much to Scott and to me as yours... and that was the Dingo. Scott and I met there. I'm sure it's here in these notebooks... 1925, sometime in the spring, I'm sure the date is here, Scott had just published *Gatsby...*" He paused as if in tribute to a book he knew might have been the best book he ever read... might've been the best book ever written... but still he couldn't quite bring himself to say it. "He was on top then and moving at top speed. Isadora Duncan lived across the street and the Dingo, bless it, was open all night. And we would meet there. It was a good time then, a polite time and it was simple and true. But I couldn't see it for what it was... or maybe I did and just held out for something more glorious."

Once his close friend, Scott was now gone, ambushed by his heart 16 years ago at 44. The gifted writer who had not only shared his money with Ernest but, in a magnanimous expression of friendship, his editor and his friends. He had given the young expatriate Ernest a running start in the race for literary promise. And what giants there were then on the left bank of the City of Light who had gone on to become literally the who's who of literature and art. And now he felt sad. Moments ago he was jubilant and now with the shadows closing in he was slipping into the dark. Was this symptomatic of what the doctors were talking about? Were these the makings of the mood swings that would seal his fate? "Be back shortly," he begged the pardon of his two friends. He walked with purpose to his room, opened the door and then closed it, sat on the fresh bed, removed his wire rims and wept.

THE CAFES

When Hemingway arrived in Cuba in the fall of '57, he was greeted by René Villarreal who had started out as a young boy at the Finca and now served as majordomo and butler. He had also grown into a confidant and friend. Old Mundo, keeper of the animals, was out looking after the cows and waved. Ernest was comfortable here, always had been, despite the fact that Castro's guerrilla operations against Batista were escalating. Cuba was his longest residence anywhere. He still could work relatively easily and well here, and now he was eager to write the book that had lain dormant and hidden in the 30 year old notebooks now stacked on his desk. The first thing he did was ask his secretary, Nita, to transcribe his journals. It took a little longer than he'd hoped but he was finally under way.

"Mary, I'm going to meet some of the pescadores at the Terraza. They heard I was back. I'll just have a rum or two and will be back soon."

"Just one or two, promise me," she said sternly. Things were not good between the two but she felt obliged to watch over his health.

"Just one or two," he nodded, knowing that was yet another promise to Mary, his fourth and final wife, he would break. It seemed broken promises came more often now. "Some who were around when we were filming the *Old Man*."

"Remember you want to be okay in the morning so you can get to work." When he worked on his Paris book there was less time for mischief and bad moods.

"I do. I do want to be fresh in the cool morning and I will work."

"I haven't seen you this eager to work in some time."

"The notebooks bring it all back, it was a good time, a young time—in ways, a foolish time—but so worth living and so worth remembering. The notes are like an echo. My memory is not near what it was, but seeing the past in my own handwriting is a good way to remember. With some luck I can smell Paris and taste it and even hear some of it. I can damn near be there. My life is played out in front of me. I am that old me," he smiled "or that young me, and I want the readers to walk the streets I walked, I want them to be there in the '20s—maybe Paris's finest years... the jazz age, the flapper era, the roaring '20s. It didn't always roar for me, but the times were extraordinary and I was learning who I was."

"I know Papa... I know," she tried being sympathetic.

"So I'm going to the Terraza. I'm going to take a rum and I'll be back. I'll have René take me. I want to see Anselmo and some of the others. I'll be back soon."

"Yes, I know, you already told me you were going," she said with no inflection in her voice.

"Well, if I did I don't remember," he said as he turned to leave the room, worrying as he did, because for some time now he was forgetting far more than he was remembering.

It was three hours later when he returned under the influence of more than the two rums he'd promised. René just shrugged when he led him into the living room. Mary shook her head and pursed her lips.

"Hi Kitten," he slurred with hollow eyes and a rubbery face. He knew better than to argue. Things had not been good for some time now. They were both trying to keep the keel even.

"I'm glad you're back."

"I met an interesting young lad. You would have liked him... would have felt soft about him. He's new to the crowd. They all sort of take care of him. He's a nice kid, always offering to help. He's a bit tardy, I'm afraid, but a wonderful kid—maybe a chapter or two behind. We talked tonight and he would ask me questions and I would answer and sometimes he'd say, "Huh?" And when he did, he really meant it. I'm going to bed now so I'll be fresh tomorrow so I can write in the cool blue light of the morning."

"Yes Papa—it's time."

"I'm going to write about Gertrude tomorrow."

"That will be larger than life I expect."

"Yes... she always was. I've already written a piece comparing two cafés and how I could write in one and not the other. But it's a short sketch—maybe 1800 words. Miss Stein will demand much more. She always did."

At the first sight of the notebooks—the same that the Paris schoolchildren had used then—he knew this was his next book. There it was, literally served up by two waiters in the office of Charley Ritz. A memoir made to order. Essays from him to him—a readymade tale that would publish and sell. The research had been done, the meticulous notes had been written in pencil over many days and nights and years, in the Parisian haunts of the budding talent that had left wherever they had come from to make their pilgrimage to the City of Light, literature and literati. With luck, the final product, he thought, would now be more a job of editing since the writing had been done. But then there was always Hadley's warning, "What we see, often depends on what we're looking for."

Now he was at his desk on a hill in San Francisco de Paula, 15 miles east of the political distractions in Havana, and ready to begin, to begin in earnest. It was all very readable now, so he dug in. It was a little hypnotic for him, to put himself back there—as if in a time machine—and the remembering was addictive. He read. He decided to read about one subject and then write a chapter about it. There was so much captivating material, that if he was not careful, he would have read it all before writing anything; and, with his memory behaving like it was, he would have to make notes on his notes before he began writing. It would be a waste of time. An outline would suffice. The first pages were about some of the cafés where these journals had been created. Good place to start, which he had learned from his old newspaper training. The who was him, the what was the sketches, the where was the cafés.

He had made his home here in Cuba since 1939. He liked writing here. Most of the time he wrote at his desk; sometimes when his back bothered him, he would stand with his typewriter elevated, surrounded by a sea of books, international taxidermy trophies and, what had become over the years, significant artwork.

As he started reading, he was unexpectedly married again to Hadley and had baby Bumby as a continual consideration. From a lifetime of writing about events still fresh in his own timeline, this retrospective filled him with images that were sometimes more like ghosts. In fact when he surveyed those in the chronicles he found that all but a few were no longer alive. This fact would make writing the book far less risky.

The Paris book would be therapeutic, in fact an alternate title might have been Paris Nostalgia. He would write about the weather and food and drink and hunger and poverty and all the things he encountered as a promising, young expat in search of a career living on his young wife's inheritance. There would be a cast of some dozen characters and critics later would divide them into the good guys and the bad guys. And he would use his iceberg technique, where the thing not mentioned or not shown garners much attention. He would write a biography or autobiography by reflection or remate (a reflective jai alai shot). In this book he would shine an analytical, examining spotlight on many others but avoid direct self-inspection and be presented in the light reflecting from the other characters. He had characterized his short, direct, clipped sentences of the '20s as writing like the Bible reads. Much of this book, too, would be written in that cadence.

"I remember this place," he thought while reading about a cafe where he drank sometimes, which was more just a place to get out of the Paris winter cold than it was a pleasant place to drink. "I didn't like the place because it was crowded with drunks and questionable women who were called a French word that basically meant female rummies. They were cheap drunks and on the make, and I disliked them as much as the cold rains of autumn that would usher in winter. The cold, wet Paris weather was very uncomfortable and we would duck into a café just to avoid it. The city became sad and dark when it was besieged by the first cold rains, or was I using the inclemency as an excuse to buy a whiskey?"

It bothered him not a little that perhaps he was now turning into that Paris that was sad and dark. "Is this me, am I this Paris? Have I become sad and dark and inclement and uncomfortable?" He wondered. He was afraid he knew the answer.

"When we first moved to Paris in 1921, sometimes the cafés, as well as my own miniature apartment, were not conducive to writing so I took a small minaret room in the hotel where Verlaine had died. It was at 39 rue Descartes around the corner from our flat on Cardinal Lemoine. Then we went to Toronto for a matter of months before we returned to Paris with Bumby between us. He had great lungs which made even a noisy café seem quieter.

"But the crowded café with the *poivrottes* and the noise also smelled bad. So I went to another café I had knowledge of on the Place Saint-Michel which was clean and warm and friendly, had a much better bouquet and was void of old women on the make drinking too much rum. I was trying to write a story about being a boy in Michigan and I had ordered a coffee. In the story, the boys are drinking, so I decided to follow up my coffee with a rum which made me warmer than the coffee. Then a young woman came into the café, and the sight of her warmed me more than the rum. So I ordered another. Now as I sit here in Cuba reading the old journals and starting to write a new story, I had the feeling that long ago all of Paris belonged to me and I had belonged to my pencil and writing pads. I had looked up from my Michigan story, and the girl was gone and I was sad. Good Lord, hasn't that always been the case. I would get busy writing, look up, and the girls would be gone… Adrienne, Hadley, Pauline and Martha. Poof. But I didn't get sad until later," he thought, "and there would always be a pretty girl for punctuation. It made no difference where it was, what country or what language. There was invariably a charming mademoiselle and for every such woman there was some chap who was tired of her, too used to her or bored, someone who was looking elsewhere. These were situations designed for trouble, anxiety and failure."

Then he read about himself ordering oysters and white wine at the warm café in Paris. "They weren't anywhere near as good as Charley's oysters, nor was the wine. But back then I didn't know enough to tell the difference. We were poor and I rarely went to the Ritz." The Paris notes were filled with menu selections.

"The short story, of course, I remember well, was *Up in Michigan,* and I had set it in Horton Bay which was close to our summer cottage. We went to Michigan in the summers and it was quite a journey. We took the steamboat out of Chicago to Harbor Springs on Little Traverse Bay, then by train to Petosky and another train to Walloon Lake Village and finally a boat across Walloon Lake to our cottage. I knew when I was writing it that it would raise most eyebrows back there, what with Jim Gilmore fondling Liz and then, worse, sort of forcing himself on her and then having the pitiful manners to pass out on top of her. I guess the good news was that they were in the missionary position—what is that page one in the Kama Sutra—nothing too wild for Midwest sensibilities. But Liz Coates, maybe I chose that name after the second St. James rum, has the magnanimity to cover the louse Jim with her coat. What does this story tell me about me when I was writing it? Paris was cold and rainy, and I was in a nice warm café. Jim and two of his buddies had some drinks, so I thought it was a good idea. Jim sees Liz. I see the gal sitting at a table by herself in the café. Normally the cafés were too noisy to do any writing as was our flat after Bumby arrived... so was I in the café to write, or was I in the café to see the young ladies?"

Ernest was 22 when he wrote *Up in Michigan* in 1921. He and Hadley moved to Toronto in 1923, had a son, and moved back to Paris in January 1924.

"In these notes I am basically describing a map of Paris, at least a map of my Paris: the bus terminal, the Café des Amateurs, the rue Mouffetard, small and narrow before it steeply rises toward La Place Contrascarpe. I guess I was taking the reader on a walking tour of the left bank, but it starts to sound too much like an atlas. I was trying to set the readers' compass. The Latin Quarter, the south side of the Seine, the Fifth Arrondissement, was an old working-class district where we first lived. It was a place for us to start out and I guess I thought it would be the same for the reader. Our apartment door was blue with a horizontal brass handle. I can see it if I close my eyes. I can see it even if I don't. We had a baby, lived in a peasant neighborhood on a tight budget, but we had the time of our lives. Our mattress was good, we had an armoire, a bowl and pitcher, a slop jar and not much else. With the apartment came a very pleasant woman, Marie Cocotte, who cleaned and polished the floor with a heavy blue flannel foot rag." He smiled at the memory. "She cooked food for us that we could eat later. There was a bedroom, a small dining room and the tiniest of kitchens. There were a lot of drunkards in the neighborhood and coal dust was everywhere. There was a small fireplace in the bedroom. Marie would empty the slop jar and fill the water pitcher. The neighborhood people were very nice to us. After dinner we would go down to the park and sit on the benches, and the sailors would ask Hadley to dance. We had a neighbor who played the accordion not much better, but not quite as loud, as Ezra had played the oboe or the bassoon or whatever instrument he was using to help him compose his opera. We were strangers in Paris so Maria and her husband Tonton would show and tell us where to go. But it didn't take long for us to learn Paris and to become part of the city. We loved life there, and it loved us back.

BONJOUR MISS STEIN

It was 7 AM in the red tiled, sun-splashed dining room. A small herd of antelope heads stared in silence from above Miro's "Finca" that hung over the buffet on the whitewashed wall. He had just eaten a slice of toast with blackberry jam someone had sent them from Maine. He knew once but could not remember who, but it had been a gift, and something delicious in a jar showed up periodically with a note. One thing about having three homes, he was never sure anymore what was where or who was sending what. With the state of his memory, one house was more than a challenge. He finished his strong Cuban coffee and Maine flavored toast. He smiled. The filters for Cuban coffee were long and narrow. Once when the last one had been used, René employed one of his new socks. It worked fine. Ernest walked to the bathroom to weigh in. His nearsightedness forced the use of his wire rims to see the numbers. He stepped on, adjusted the counterweights and let the bar settle.

"Damn," he swore at the two pounds. He took the pencil from the top of the three shelf bookcase and wrote the new number on the wall. It was his weight or his blood pressure or his diet or his drinking. Something was always out of range or breaking down. It was never good news and it worried him. The doctors, the white coats, would be concerned. Their new words were "in decline" and "deteriorating". He knew he was running aground. He knew he was not in good shape. He looked at the hundred or so books in the low white bookcase. There was one from Turgenev that he had first read in Paris—from the very early days in Paris. Sylvia Beach had lent it to him, and had not made him pay the library fee. He was habitually broke and she trusted him for it. When he got home Hadley, who enforced a strict code of conduct, made him march back and pay with the money he had been saving for a whiskey. It reminded him of his father, who had also made him responsible for library fines for books that they took to Walloon Lake in the summers.

He smiled a weak but pleasant smile and walked out into a glorious West 23° latitude, 70° day. He walked to the pool past the graves of some of his cats and sat on the chaise. The water in the pool was clear and looked cool. The pergola was above the circular steps of the pool where Ava Gardner, who had told him, "Deep down I'm pretty superficial", sat once without her bathing suit. That was one memory he didn't have difficulty recalling. There had been a sound stage full of Hollywood people he counted as friends who had been to the Finca, but his two favorites were Gary Cooper and Ava Gardner. "Coops" had become a real hunting companion in Idaho and a friend for 12 years. He smiled again remembering how Cooper used to insist on sleeping in the library when he visited. Ava was a favorite for a few reasons. Ernest referred to her as a long stemmed beauty and she was. Her career had taken off with her 1946 portrayal of Kitty in Hemingway's "The Killers". He introduced her to bullfighting and she became a big fan. He also introduced her to Dominguin and she became a bigger fan. A very special fan. The beautiful actress and the celebrated matador had done a little bullfighting of their own. Sitting there letting the morning sun warm him, he thought of Ava resting naked like one of Pascin's models, without speaking, a silent siren beautiful to see, on the steps of the pool. He also remembered when Adriana Ivancich had visited almost 10 years ago. Mary had watched her like a famished hawk. "So did I," he thought. He had fallen for the Venetian charmer. He felt foolish now looking back. "I was an old fool chasing a school girl delicacy." He had gifted her a typewriter to write him letters and an expensive Rolleiflex for her to take pictures to send to him. "I was a pig to Mary," he remembered with a good degree of guilt. He had called her names, scurrilous names, in front of other people and had actually thrown a drink in her face. He closed his eyes and shook his head. He had acted the ass as he had done many times before. In fact, boorish behavior and Ernesto were not strangers. The one bright memory was that he had started writing the *Old Man and the Sea* at that time in his life.

He rose, kicked off his sandals and sat with his feet on the first step of the pool. The water was like the morning, cool and refreshing. He thought Adriana was his muse and that she had inspired his writing. When she left they wrote. He would meet her again at different times in Italy. They had flirted with sexual situations but none satisfactory to the old man. Sitting here in Cuba he still felt regret at that, though he did manage a nude photograph—albeit from the back. Good enough for some nights. Perhaps he would not have missed her quite as much, there with his feet in the water and his head in the past, if he could have known that five years after his death she would sell his letters to a New York book dealer for $17,000 at Christie's and hang herself from a tree in her front yard in Capalbio, Tuscany. He sat staring into the clear, blue green. It was going to be another beautiful day in San Francisco de Paula. He wondered how many more there would be. He thought again about the women, about Adriana and the others. Sex had always been a big part of what drove him. He had many appetites, and this one was serious. He had learned about it, performed it, dreamt about it, bragged about it, wore out three wives with it, but now he just remembered it. There were captivating memories, even potent memories, but memories nonetheless. The first sex he had written about was *Up in Michigan*, Jim Gilmore and Liz Coates. He used to know how many copies of the story were printed in Paris and by whom. He used to use it as a test to see how drunk he was. He would never again recall that it was 300 by Robert McAlmon in 1923. At 24 he was young, vibrant and knew as much about sex as any red blooded young man his age. But his first instruction, his first formal schooling came when Miss Stein enlightened him in Paris. There were notes in his Paris papers. This peculiar guidance deserved a chapter.

He left the pool and walked to the desk in his bedroom. There were the notebooks, the transcriptions, his Royal typewriter and packages of paper. He was ready. The portable Corona that Hadley had given him for his 22nd birthday was downstairs. What typing he had managed in Paris had been hammered out on that typewriter. Perhaps that machine was more fitting for the Paris book. He scanned the notes he had organized into the Paris memoir he was culling from the past.

"Well, I introduced the reader to my neighborhood and then I went skiing in Switzerland. Perhaps I should take them back to Paris and begin introducing them to the expats who had gathered there. I think I'll start with Gertrude, after all she was my mentor and patron early on. She opened her address book to me, introduced me around and really got me started. She sponsored me. Miss Stein and I became friends. We spent time together. I took black-and-white photos of her on the gravel paths at Luxembourg Gardens with Bumby, Alice, Hadley and Gertrude. You can see my shadow cast in front of me in the pictures, sun behind, as I took the photos. Gertrude and Alice were Bumby's godparents. They made an odd couple. Gertrude was a very large person, Alice was wispy. If Gertrude's existence was convoluted, Alice's was simple and direct. Alice called her partner 'the mother of us all'.

"We came back from skiing to a Parisian winter. The modest fireplace in our bedroom made the small apartment warm and cheerful. Thanks to my painting friends, I saw most things as an artist. The winter light was beautiful and the bare trees were sculptures. In my small turret around the corner, I would splurge with firewood, tangerines and chestnuts. It doesn't sound like much as I sit here today, but then they seemed like riches. I stuck to my rule of writing until I had something finished and would stop when I knew what was going to happen next. That way there would be no start up time the next day, no delay. I could hit the ground running. When starting something new, and I have written this more than once, the trick was to write one true sentence. It was easier then, there was always one good sentence somewhere that I knew or had seen someplace or had heard someone say or listened to in a song.

"In Paris, when I had stopped working for the newspaper and we were living on Hadley's inheritance, my vocation—such as it was—was writing. When I would finish writing for the day, my avocation was to walk anywhere in Paris that I could get to comfortably. When I had finished walking past the shops, in and out of the cafés or into a museum or two, I would many times wind up at 27 rue de Fleurus, the studio of Gertrude Stein.

"Hadley and I would go. Gertrude and Alice were still friendly to us then. We were strangers in their city but we were gaining on it. At Miss Stein's, we loved the art, we loved the fire and the food, we loved her cordials made from assorted fruits. Miss Stein had small eyes somewhat lost in a wide peasant face. Miss Toklas had short dark hair, a very large hooked nose and was frightening. They were generous to us then but when we invited them to our small apartment for tea, it did not go that well. Miss Stein sat on our bed and read some of my stories but did not like the one about Jim and Liz. It put her off, she was not pleased and she labeled it *inaccrochable*. She explained that this is a term used when a painting was unacceptable for any reason. It was not worth hanging, or un-hangable or *inaccrochable*. So sitting there on our bed in our apartment she determined that my story was distasteful. She saw the Michigan story as too controversial for its time. I have to admit to similar feelings. She had judged that Jim Gilmore's fondling and sexual conquest of Liz would be too shocking for the folks up in Michigan, or most places in the U.S. for that matter, to accept. And it was. There were folks I knew in Horton Bay who were upset. Jim Gilmore in my story was a blacksmith. Jim Dilworth owned a blacksmith shop in Horton Bay and resembled Jim Gilmore. He was not happy. His wife's name was Elizabeth. She was also not a fan of the story. I do admit to being surprised at the time at the expat reaction because I thought Paris, with its more liberal view of most everything, would be more understanding, more accepting. So to hear Miss Stein say it shouldn't be published, was not what I expected. Not what I had wanted to hear. She called the story silly. She said it was wrong and silly and there was no point in writing a story like that.

"But if I didn't agree with her about *Up in Michigan*, I did agree with her advice about buying art. She told me to buy artists my own age, not the Cezannes and early Matisses and Picassos that hung on her walls but from the expat crowd living there, like Miro and Masson, the new artists who someday might be famous. She knew of what she spoke.

"She made it clear to me then, that I was invited to visit her studio not only at the salons held on Saturday evenings but also any afternoon after five. I would do so quite often and drank from her collection of cognacs. Sometimes her cognacs were almost as fascinating as her collection of art. She showed me her writing, which was more experimental than not. I did not sit on her bed. I did not say that her work was distasteful. I did not label it *inaccrochable*. I thought that perhaps she hadn't put enough effort into making her writing intelligible. But it was a silent thought I did not share with the author or her companion. I did volunteer to proofread her material, a task as laborious as it was valuable to our relationship. It was like plowing a wet field; and, although she was grateful for the proofreading, she judged that I had other shortcomings, which she enumerated without compunction. Perhaps the most puzzling of these was the knowledge gap she claimed I had when it came to sex.

"This was thin ice. I have to admit to harboring a prejudice against homosexuality in the 1920s in Paris and Miss Stein was a lesbian. I had spoken in front of her almost too easily about being able to hurt anyone threatening me in that regard. Interestingly, Miss Stein degraded males of that persuasion but claimed females in that category did nothing that disgusted them and afterwards they were happy. That sounded to me as experimental as some of her writing. It also seemed quite a bit more distasteful and *inaccrochable* than my short story.

"Perhaps I can use these walks around Paris as a way to introduce characters in the next chapter. For example if I left Miss Stein's apartment on the rue de Fleurus, I could walk along the rue de Vaugirard, the longest street in Paris, where Scott and Zelda lived at number 58. Miss Stein did not live that far away from the Fitzgeralds, and soon I would introduce them—a move that added to both my admiration and hostility toward Scott."

Ernest's writing schedule was to work in the morning and when he'd crafted something he liked, he'd use the afternoon for recreation, usually fishing or entertaining guests or answering letters. Yesterday afternoon he'd gone to the art museum in Havana. He liked Cuban art and Cuban artists, from Victor

Manuel's "Tropical Gypsy" to the ghost-like canvasses of Antonia Eiriz. They had arrived home early, had dinner and wine and were not late to bed. He awoke without a hangover. On other mornings when he was less fortunate and Mary would offer him an Alka-Seltzer, he would decline, complaining that the noise was too loud.

THE LOST GENERATION

He was at his bedroom desk with the big typewriter. It was early, the Cuban sun was just rising. Mundo had been tending the cows that would soon become a state monopoly. Ernest was alone with a pot of coffee and had finished arranging some of his 30-year-old notes on Miss Stein. He wanted to write one entire chapter on her without stopping. He took a deep remembrance breath and began.

"Gertrude Stein, as I have said, was not small of stature but rather large, not unlike some athletes I have seen playing football. She was big enough that all of her is not going to fit into one chapter. So I'll just pick up where I left off and continue with the tribal dance that Miss Stein and I managed for quite a while. As I have said, I was welcome, at least initially, to stop by her studio in the afternoons after 5 o'clock. But this would change, as our friendship had been marked for death. As I look at it today, through a 30 year lens, the tumultuous ending could've been avoided. In those days, after writing for the day if I couldn't do one of a number of things I really enjoyed, like making love or drinking in a café, I would read. Since I mapped out geography in the last chapters, perhaps I should begin mapping literature, or at least talk about the authors I was reading when I couldn't roll in our bed near the fireplace next to the living room with shiny floors. But listing authors is a lot like collecting all the books that line the Finca—it screams look at me; and as I sit here flirting with mortality, it seems I could have done a lot less screaming over the years. Sylvia Beach had recommended a lot of good authors to me and since she had the books on loan, I could take them out and read them. But here again Miss Stein and I disagreed on who was a good author and who was not. She did not like Huxley for example. She called his writing trash, in fact her words were "inflated trash by a dead man". Not exactly high praise. She didn't like DH Lawrence any better, calling him pathetic and preposterous and accusing him of writing like a sick man—sick in the moral sense. So here's an old butch lying with another woman in 1920, and she thinks DH Lawrence is off-color. Something was amiss. She recommended Marie Belloc Lowndes, an English novelist whose work I enjoyed, especially *The Lodger*—a tale of Jack the Ripper. Lowndes was a prolific English novelist raised in France. She averaged a published work a year and that's when you know you're running at top speed. She wrote a memoir of her mother's life compiled from old family letters and memories of her early days in France. I guess it wasn't all that different from what I'm trying to do now.

"Miss Stein and I were good friends for maybe four years. She spoke well of Scott Fitzgerald and Ron Firbank who was an openly gay, innovative English novelist inspired by Oscar Wilde. They even looked somewhat alike, that is Wilde and Firbank, although of an early morning in bad light you might add Miss Stein to that mix. She also liked Sherwood Anderson as a person but never spoke of his writing. She liked the work of Firbank and Scott, but since she hadn't mentioned the work of Anderson, I thought maybe his writing was at least suspect in her mind. Wrong. I made a grievous miscalculation when I went after Sherwood Anderson. I think I knew better but I did it anyway. I was ready to tell her how bad his novels were even though I knew he was one of her most loyal fans, and if there was one thing Miss Stein valued it was loyalty. But when Anderson wrote *Dark Laughter,* a 1925 novel about sexual freedom in the '20s, I let him have it. I took some serious shots at him in *Torrents of Spring* that came out in 1926. I aped his book. It was not kind. Hadley called it nasty. Miss Stein strongly objected to it, which is to say she blew her stack especially since Anderson had helped me get published. She said it was unforgivable and in retrospect, it was. The friendship between the Steins and the Hemingways came to an end. And that, as they say, was squarely on my shoulders.

"So here I was, a married man with a son, who at least felt

confident enough to broach sex in this Michigan story. I was not unaccustomed to the bedroom. And I'm in Paris, City of Light and other things and not uninitiated when it came to the ladies of the evening and I felt myself being instructed in sexuality by an outsized lesbian with a flying monkey for a girlfriend. Now there's a twist.

"No matter how you look at it, Gertrude and Alice were characters with a capital C, especially for the early 1920s. Sometimes they appeared as pastiches of themselves. Miss Stein had serious wealth and all the art and other finery and connections that went with it. She was also an author of novels, plays and poetry—experimenting in that part of her life also. She was a force—the center of gravity in the expat community. What was I thinking? She was a young writer's dream. She had been in Paris since 1903 and had met her lifelong partner in 1907, on Alice's first day in Paris. It was love at first sight. Gertrude began introducing her to her friends, the first being Picasso at his *Le Bateau Lavoir* studio. This boat wash house was the sobriquet for a rather poor excuse for a building in Montmartre. On stormy days the building would sway and creak in the wind, reminding whoever named the building of the sounds of washing the boats on the nearby Seine. It became famous as the residence for many artists of the period. Its curious name was coined by a French artist Max Jacob who at one time had been Picasso's roommate and who taught the Spaniard French. He was also a good friend of Modigliani. At this time Picasso was painting *Le Bordel d'Avignon,* a good-sized oil depicting five young, nude prostitutes from a Barcelona brothel. The women are angular; and, quite frankly scare the hell out of most people. At the painting's first exhibition in 1916, it was said to be immoral. I always wondered if Picasso got the same *inaccrochable* speech from Miss Stein that I did. But I'm not so sure being 'unhangable' was still a bad thing. Rich people would buy immoral and his painting was revolutionary and eventually led to the Cubist movement. As I sit here reading my notes it looks like I'm excusing myself somewhat when I say that Miss Stein was angry with me, but she was also mad at Ezra Pound, as if her being mad at Ezra somehow made my actions okay. Ezra had broken one of her chairs and I had broken one of her friends, but I insinuate it was her fault that she was mad at me. I don't think so now, but I wrote it then, so I'll write it now.

"Somewhat out of sequence the notes tell the story of how the phrase 'lost generation' came about. I would have remembered this one without my notes. It was during the second stay in Paris that began in January 1924 when I was assisting Ford Madox Ford in editing the *Transatlantic Review*—which was publishing, among others, Miss Stein. At this point we were still friends, when she came up with the designation "lost generation". It was like Scott coming up with the term "Jazz age", inventing either one of those labels put you in the sobriquet hall of fame. It all had to do with the old Lizzie Ford she was driving and the kid, who had served in the war, who was now servicing her car at the local garage. For some reason Miss Stein was not satisfied—she was not satisfied a lot—with the young man or his work. When she was not satisfied, no one was. She wasn't happy till everyone wasn't happy. The garage owner, taking the wealthy customer's side, condemned not only the lad but his entire, postwar age group worldwide when he said 'you are all a generation perdu'. Well, that did it, we were all—all of us, myself included, who served in the war—part of this lost generation. With one offhanded pronouncement from a car repair man, we were all branded for life. Then she went on to claim that we had no respect for anything and that we were all a bunch of drunkards. I couldn't really argue with the latter part of that condemnation. But as I sit here today, quite far from Paris in space and time, I think one of the few people who deserved that label was the woman who coined it.

"I think I remember drinking whiskeys, and I don't wish to hazard a guess as to the number, when I was writing the next part of this journal. I was trying to explain how I tried to balance her lost generation quote with my book's title from the first chapter of *Ecclesiastes,* verse five, 'the sun also rises, and the sun goes down, and hastens to the place where he arose'. What I was trying to say was that a generation, lost or not, goes and another generation comes. The sun rises and the sun sets with a promise to rise again. There is hope. It's the promise to rise again that I was after. That's the message: optimism, peace under pressure, hope. But then, and I think this is where the whiskey kicked in, in the next sentence I quickly turned and talked about my knowledge of ambulance drivers. Because I have been getting so forgetful, it makes me feel a little better, that I can remember Ted Brumbach from the Kansas City Star who got me interested in ambulance driving. But now it seems to be another, look at me, sentence. Then I banged around Miss Stein and Sherwood Anderson one more time for good measure citing their egotism and mental laziness and tagged them with the lost generation label.

"In the notebooks I finish the sketch by completing my walk. I really don't remember why I thought walking instructions were so necessary, perhaps trying to put the reader literally in my footsteps. At any rate I approached the Lilas Café and across the street saw the statue of Marshall Ney, one of Napoleon's 18 marshals of the Empire, known for his bravery. I call the statue Mike Ney as if the dead soldier was a friend of mine. It was either the whiskey or my rather pitiful desire to be accepted by my newly adopted city, or both, that shows through here. After Napoleon's defeat and exile, Ney was arrested, tried and found guilty of treason and executed in a profound miscarriage of justice. He was put to death by firing squad. He refused to wear the customary blindfold. He was permitted to give the order to fire and reportedly said something like I have fought 100 battles for France and not one against her and then ordered the soldiers to fire. By God that's courage. Ney's failure at Waterloo made me think that all generations were lost so I stopped in the café for a cold beer and remembered Ney's battlefield bravery and Miss Stein's eulogy of Guillaume Apollinaire, one of her favorite French writers and art critics, who had died on November 9, 1918—the day of the armistice of the first world war. He had an almost fanciful existence. First of all his name was Wilhelm Albert Wlodzimierz Apolinary Kostrowicki. He coined the terms cubism and surrealism—either one would have put you in Who's Who. He was accused of stealing the Mona Lisa from the Louvre, which would also put you in Who's Who. The thief turned out to be some Italian house painter who was caught trying to sell it in Florence. Apollinaire was severely wounded in the war and died at age 38 during the Spanish influenza epidemic or pandemic or whatever the hell you call it. One of his best quotes for me was something like now and then it's good to pause in our pursuit of happiness and just be happy. There's one to have a drink over.

"As I read these notes I see that more than once I tried to excuse my loss of Miss Stein's friendship. Even then I must've known it was a huge mistake. I was literally biting the hand that fed my family. I praised her, then cursed her as if to tell myself it's okay that we were no longer friends and I finish with some weak claim that yes, she is nice but that she does talk trash at times. I had to be drinking, but I did not take a shot at Miss Toklas, the wife in their household arrangement. Perhaps I feared she would stalk my dreams."

THE BOOKSTORE

Yesterday he had started and finished a short chapter on Gertrude Stein. He was proud of himself and he should've been. "Damn," he said, "they've been counting me down, maybe this will change things a little." But something had occurred to him while he was working. He has all these valuable notes, sketches and stories from a great time in his life. Enough to construct the book. He had recorded what was taking place around him like the reporter he was. It was good material and would work well. But now he had a question for himself. He realized as he wrote that he had a 30 year advantage on his journals. Now he knew more, much more. He was the future now and he knew how events had unfolded, which gambles had paid off, who wound up sleeping with or loving or marrying whom, who were still friends, who had become famous and who were still alive. How should this affect his book? Or should it? Should he blank it out completely? The answer had to be yes—but was it possible? It would be interesting to be sure. It would be difficult, certainly, to be the omniscient narrator who really was omniscient, who really did know more than the 1920s characters—the panoptical chronicler who had lived the future that the Jazz Age Parisians had only dreamt about and that he had recorded so carefully 30 years ago in the cafés and cold water flats. He would use his notes and write it the way it happened so long ago. This was five years in Paris of another age and that report had to be true and authentic and as correct as he could make it, so that there would be an account of how it was so long ago in the City of Light when he was young and alive and learning to be the writer he had become.

It was 9 AM. He had been up since six. There were coffee and toast and a sweet roll left over from yesterday. He put jam on the toast and vowed not to eat the roll, but did anyway. The self-control on which he had falsely prided himself for years, was gone. His diabetes demanded he keep his weight down, but he was ballooning. The doctors were worried. He was worried. The discipline that he used to derive from hunger was gone. His Paris journals were full of examples of how hunger made him a better writer, a better observer of the arts. No more. Those days were well gone as was the health he had taken for granted. Mary had dragged Hotch off into Havana to a breakfast that Ernest had promised to attend months ago. But he was having one of his black ass days; and, depressed, he didn't want to go. He didn't want to be with a lot of people—he didn't even want to be with a few people. Mary would tell them he was truly sorry, that he was working on a book, and the check she carried would make them feel better. He had also sent autographed copies of *Old Man*.

He was happy for the silence in the Finca. René and the others had the ability to disappear and only appear, wraith-like, if he needed them. He had tried to work this morning but with no luck. He had left off yesterday, after 500 words, with an idea of what to write next, but his old strategy had failed. Maybe a different stimulus would help—the phonograph. He liked listening to Louis Armstrong and some of the records Marlena Dietrich had sent him, but not this morning. He didn't feel like doing much of anything this morning, but a tune had been playing in his head lately, a French tune, probably brought on by the work he was doing. Maybe it was the Paris book, all the Parisian sketches, the memories from one of his favorite cities. Whatever it was, it kept repeating in his mind's ear. It was by Édith Piaf. Listening to her, sounded like the Paris of 30 years ago. It even brought to mind the *bal musette* below their apartment above the saw mill. She wasn't singing then of course, she wasn't born until 1915 but her voice and her song somehow matched what he was feeling. They called her the little sparrow which fit her small features and her pencil thin eyebrows. She sang many great French songs but the one repeating in his old concussed head was a new song, "Milord" with its almost honky-tonk chorus. If his French held, the *chanson* was about a lower-class girl who falls for an upper-class Brit. She sees him walking with another woman but he doesn't notice her. She feels that she is a mere shadow on the street but when she talks to him of love, things change. He cries and she cheers him up. It's the chorus that finds Ernest humming. It also reminded him of the music a young lad played on the street with an accordion in front of Sylvia Beach's bookstore. The kind heart that she was, she would feed him occasionally and he would get tips from the patrons that could afford it. Today he would write about Miss Beach.

"There weren't many people who were nicer to me than Sylvia Beach. She was an American, a minister's daughter, known for her Paris bookstore, Shakespeare and Company. She lobbied for the 1923 publication of my first book, *Three Stories and 10 Poems* and sold it in her shop. Sylvia is probably best known for publishing Joyce's *Ulysses* in 1922. We both owed her. She lived with her lover Adrienne Monnier, who, ironically, owned a nearby bookstore until her death in 1955. I think Sylvia was attracted to me even though she didn't take men as lovers and I notice in my journals that I spent entirely too much time on this subject. I liked both her and her partner. As noted they both owned shops on rue Odeon.

"Books were almost as important to me as food. As a youngster my eyesight was not perfect, in fact it kept me out of the war, but now, like the rest of me, my eyes are deteriorating. I wish I had the vision of Gregorio. We're about the same age but he has blue, undefeated eyes and his peripheral vision for sighting marlins is extraordinary. I swear on a good day he can see his own laugh lines.

Anyway my vision and my coordination were not top-flight. I would have great difficulty following the flight of a ball, no matter what kind it was. So I took up fishing and shooting and boxing in which there was no ball to follow. I found out early in life that I did not like exhibiting my awkwardness on a sports field and that my left eye dominated my right, but was too vain to wear glasses. That's when I found out that there is no friend as loyal as a book. I was not so good at sports but I became very good at reading. In my notes I had jotted down a sentence stating that life was my sport, but I think that's a bit overdone so it will not make it into the chapter. So Sylvia's bookstore became very important to me not only as a source for great books but also as a meeting spot for a lot of people I wanted to know. It was warm, all the really good places were warm, and there was a large stove that made it cheery. She let me borrow books before I had joined. She trusted people. I borrowed the Russians—Turgenev's collection of short stories, Tolstoy's *War and Peace* and some of Dostoevsky's short stories. I also took along Lawrence's *Sons and Lovers*. Whenever I would carry out thick books or a lot of thinner ones, Sylvia would tell me that it was going to take me a long time to plow through them. She was right, but for me it was great entertainment. Some of my friends who knew much more about literature than I did at the time, would give me the context in which some of the books I was reading had been written. An example I remember was the collection of short stories Turgenev had written back in 1852. They were his own observations while hunting on his mother's estate where he witnessed the abuse of the peasants and the Russian system that made such abuse possible. He was later put under house arrest for writing the stories but he is credited with the eventual abolition of serfdom in Russia.

My two enthusiasms in Sylvia's library/bookstore were the books themselves and those who wrote them. I remember asking Sylvia when I would be likely to find James Joyce in her shop as I wanted to time my visits with his. She said late in the afternoon. I thought of my visits to Miss Stein's that took place late in the afternoon. I was used to visits late in the afternoons. Sylvia seemed surprised that I had not met him. I told her that I'd seen him at Michaud's—an expensive meal on the rue Jacob. He had been with his wife Nora, whose name before marrying James was Barnacle—a misnomer if there ever was one. She was smart and very nice and in appearance looked as though she could have been a member of the Chaplin family.

"Hadley and I, and Evan Shipman and I, had gone to the races many times at Auteuil and Enghien and for a time we won our share of races, especially when I would go with Evan who was expert at handicapping. The large hippodrome at Auteuil opened in 1873 and along with the Enghien racecourse provided good races and a fair drink. One of the times when we won, I took Hadley to Michaud's for dinner, a special event because we were spending the track's money on this one. This is where we saw Joyce and his family for the first time. I must admit I can still remember what a big deal it was for me.

"I must admit that, in reading over the journals, I had no idea I had written that much about being hungry. I must've told everybody that I didn't get enough to eat, including Sylvia. She asked me if I ate at home. I told her about Maria, the cook we had who prepared good food for us. She would come every day and, besides cleaning well, she was a very accomplished cook. Sylvia and Hadley admired each other and she invited us to dinner on several occasions. She and Adrienne ran a very comfortable household, very different in atmosphere from that of Miss Stein and Alice. When I look around at the spacious rooms of the Finca, our first apartment in Paris would have fit into one room here. In those days we had two rooms, cold water, no inside plumbing—just a slop jar. But it did have a good view and a good mattress with springs.

"There were many times when Hadley and I at the end of the day would walk along the river and window shop and then maybe stop into a café where no one knew us, and have a drink or two and then back to our flat for the dinner Marie had cooked us. In my notes it's almost like I boast that after dinner we would read and make love. But I'm not sure that's anybody's business or that anyone cares.

"I've run across several lines in these Paris sketches that hurt. Innocent enough when they were written, 30 years later they're now a shot to the heart. One was, 'and we will never love anyone else but each other'. My memory's not what it used to be, but I can remember saying this to Hadley as if it were yesterday. She sued me for divorce in 1927 but I had started loving someone else sometime before that. It was a pattern I developed. A good friend once told me that maybe the reason I left three of my wives was because I had been left by my father when I was young and I did not want that to happen again. I'll leave that to the gentlemen in the white coats.

"I also noticed that in these café notes I write out entire meals that were eaten. I can remember doing it a few times in the Lilas and maybe some of our friends would talk to us about certain dishes from time to time. There's one lunch menu, and I had a little trouble reading my own writing, which was unusual, since my handwriting was fairly readable and easily understood. But evidently this one menu that I enjoyed had a radish and endive salad, calves liver, mashed potatoes followed up by an apple tart. It says nothing about the liquid refreshment, but I'm sure that might've been the most memorable part of the lunch inasmuch as the handwriting was marginal and the pages had been soaked with liquid—odds are an alcoholic one.

"Hadley had me borrow Henry James from Sylvia's. I think James sold his books by the pound but Hadley really liked his books and his assertion that kindness is the most important thing in life. She also liked the idea that James espoused about taking an agreeable hour every afternoon and drinking tea. If she dropped the word 'tea', I could have agreed. But I shouldn't short change James, there was a lot to him, he was nominated for the Nobel three times and his development of the interior monologue technique gave Joyce a leg up."

It was quite a while before Hemingway started typing on this chapter about Sylvia Beach. He read and reread some of the transcribed notes. His favorite lines described how lucky he felt then, and how they ate and drank well and cheaply and slept well and warm together and loved each other. It seemed to make him sad, but he read them over and over. The sketches led him into reminiscence: "We were so lucky then, but I never thought to knock on wood. You would've thought that a man who carried a buckeye and a rabbit's foot would have remembered to knock on wood."

THE SEINE

"I started this chapter about the people of the Seine when I was in Idaho spending time with some of my neighbors who lived along Silver Creek. Now Silver Creek is certainly no Seine, but I think people who live on or close to the water share some traits and maybe a few dreams. Now I'm back in Cuba with another group of people who live near the water and they, too, share some of the same attitudes and ethics as the water people in Paris and Idaho. René had driven Mary and me to Cojimar and Gregorio had walked from his home on Pasuela. He lived close to both the dock and La Terraza, which would have been dangerous for me. He was on board smoking his ever-present Romeo & Juliet 7" cigar. His wife Dolores had packed him something special in a small paper bag. They had four daughters. No wonder he enjoyed going to sea, he was outnumbered. Gregorio and Mary and I were on the *Pilar* yesterday, 8 miles out, and for once I didn't have the fire in my belly to go fishing. We just cruised, not saying much, but it's important to have comfortable silences once in a while. Gregorio as always had his keen eyes on the sea and pointed to a breaching bill fish. Mary was catching some sun and reading a magazine. I was remembering the Seine and how I used to walk to it from our small apartment. The shortest route from our apartment to the Seine was right down our street, but it was steep and full of traffic until it hit an unattractive riverbank with matching warehouses that resembled prisons. The Île St. Louis, where Bill Bird had his Three Mountain Press on the *quai d'Anjou*, was a much better walk and you could cross over there and turn left along the quays and pass Île St. Louis, Notre Dame and Ile de la Cite opposite. These are the two natural islands in the Seine within the city of Paris. On my endless search for books, I would rummage through the stalls along the quays for cheap American editions. There were a few book stalls that served as unofficial lost and founds for certain establishments near the river. Some hotels and cafes would take any books left behind to be sold at certain stalls. Often they were tattered and frayed or had been the object of a spill. That's when I first found out that you couldn't tell a book by its cover… or its binding.

"Another characteristic of the Paris sketches is the speed with which I would change subjects. I'm sure some of this was a result of writing in a café, stopping and having a whiskey or two and then starting to write the next day on another subject without starting a new page. Scott and I wrote each other letters that would be written over a week or more and they suffered from the same phenomenon—the handwriting would go downhill to the right if alcohol was involved. Whatever the cause, I notice that subject changes occur rapidly and with some frequency. So I go, in this one journal, from talking about books to fishing. These have been two loves of mine for a long time: reading and fishing. The fishing in Cuba might be the best anywhere, for me at least. The fish here are Marlins and they are huge and they fight you with everything they have and you know you've done something significant when you win that battle. Freshwater fishing is something completely different but very interesting just the same. In Paris along the Seine, men fished for something just big enough to take home for dinner. Walking along the quays was good for my head, either after I had finished writing for the day or while I was trying to solve something. Fishing was also a pleasant release for me, and I found a good place to fish near the statue of King Henry IV, who had the dubious record of having a dozen assassination attempts on his life. There was a small park on the river with a great many spreading chestnuts, not like the Cuban ficus or fig but beautiful just the same. The Pont Neuf is a massive bridge that provided good fishing in its shadow. The fishermen will tell you it is the oldest bridge across the Seine and the first one to cross the river in a single span, being nearly 1000 feet long and 75 feet wide.

The fisherman there used very light gear, jointed bamboo poles and feather floats; and they would catch nice white carp and cut them into strips and deep fry them. They were not unlike the freshwater fish we caught off the dock I had written about in the Michigan story, the dock where Jim Gilmore forced himself on Liz Coates. It is a thrill for me to realize that here I have become one of the foremost bill fishermen in Cojimar—which is a feat inasmuch as this town boasts the best bill fishermen in all of Cuba if not anywhere. I've been fortunate enough to make good friends with these people. They are good and proud and honest and will do anything for you. These were the fisherman who came together in the *Old Man and the Sea*, men like Anselmo Hernandez, El Sordo, Figurin, Marcos Puig, Negro Arsenio and Santiago el Soltero and Tato and the rest of the fisherman of the deep.

"But here I am walking through the cafés in Paris taking notes, reading books, trying to write and make a living for my wife and my son. I had yet to think about the *Old Man and the Sea*. I had not begun to even dream about a Pulitzer. So many good things have happened to me, and seeing Hadley's name over and over, I realize so many not so good. But with my diseases and my shortcomings in my head that does not behave all the time, I must admit I've come a long way since walking along the river in Paris so long ago. Most of those who peopled the notebooks are gone by now. It would be a treasure to be able to see them, to catch up, to compare notes, to have a drink and swear a friendship. When I pick one of the notebooks from my desk and hold it to my nose I can still smell the antique musty scent of the Ritz cellar and, not unlike Proust with the taste of small cakes, the scent triggers a déjà vu back to a different time in the City of Light.

"As for the fish that I pulled out of the Seine, I have in my notes that I ate them fried, bones and all. I can't believe I did that. Eating fish bones is never a good idea, for man or beast… or maybe even fish for that matter. Sherwood Anderson, who would help me get published, actually died from swallowing a toothpick—not all that different from a fishbone—while on a cruise to South America. The poor bastard had evidently swallowed a toothpick while eating hors d'oeuvres or the olive from a martini. Something serious got punctured, he was diagnosed with peritonitis and died. But evidently we ate the fish, bones and all, and washed them down with a friendly white wine outside at *La Pêche Miraculeuse* on the Canal Saint-Martin, named for the miracles of the fish and the loaves. I remember Guy de Maupassant had mentioned the restaurant in a short story. The view from this place was quite pleasant and reminded me of paintings of the Seine by Alfred Sisley which are peaceful and soft and shaded with pale greens, purples blues and a little pink on occasion. It seemed to me that over the years the intensity of the colors in his paintings increased and I wondered if his vision was weakening, as mine is now, and that to him the brighter colors actually looked the same. Colors have not been the same for me for some time. A lot in my life is weakening.

"Anyway *La Pêche Miraculeuse* was expensive and Hadley and I would go there only when we had saved enough money from other pursuits or had a horse come home at one of the tracks. But there were a lot of small restaurants with good fish fries. I really didn't become involved in fishing on the Seine but I enjoyed watching the others nevertheless. Between the good and friendly fisherman and the barge community, the Seine was a busy and interesting place. The barges were floating, working pieces of art with their colors and their lively onboard existence. Something I never saw in America, where most bridges are tall, were the tugs' smokestacks that folded down in order to pass under some of the 37 bridges on the Seine. There's a lively oil by de Vlaminck of a tugboat on the Seine. The colors are strong, the painting pleasant.

"Trees held a special fascination for me, still do. I notice in my notes that I used the trees as harbingers for the seasons. In Paris they were chestnuts, elms, poplars that I used, sometimes daily, for tokens of spring that would ride in on a warm wind one morning—I remember writing that, it's a good word picture. Sometimes the weather cheated spring's tenancy and we would endure what I called a false spring. I was elegiac about the loss of a good season. The proposition of spring, like Miss Stein, was very considerable and my Paris notes look at spring from so many angles that, like her, it will probably play a part in more than one chapter. I learned a long time ago not to forget to put weather in a story."

The poetry of his speech and the images from Paris, still alive in his ebbing imagination, gripped him with sadness and a longing to be the way he used to be. Sadder still was the knowledge that he never again would be that way; in fact never again would he be as good as he was today. From here each day would start slowly and taper off. He knew he had to gird himself for the ill-fated battle that lay ahead. He couldn't afford to lose much more ground too quickly. His journal, his gallery, his Paris book were for him a black and white film of the left bank in the '20s that he was narrating. He would try to keep the film on the reels for as long as he could. It was very important to him and; he thought, probably to his health, to finish this Paris word painting. He had noticed in the Paris sketches that there was a lot of hunger and death as a backdrop. He thought he might have used both too much.

THE WEATHER

He woke up in one of the twin beds in the long narrow bedroom of the Finca with the ubiquitous overstuffed bookcases. It was the day after Christmas 1957 and there was a tree downstairs about 6 feet tall with candles. Siskie was there and the Richards girls and, of course, René, Juan the chauffeur and Pichilo the gardener. Christmas music was coming from the oversized portable Zenith radio and Ernest was feeling okay—not great—but well enough to work. He had drunk last night and he had drunk too much. The doctors knew better and had told him to moderate. Mary knew better and wished he would stop. He knew better and pledged not to be over-served or to over celebrate. He also knew it was an empty pledge. He didn't need the Paris journals he was reading to remind him that he had always had issues with his whiskey and his wine and his beer and his cognac. In fact alcohol, in more forms than he remembered, had played a starring role in some of his expat dramas. He was not alone in this accomplishment, and had even been outdone by several of his running mates. Devil rum had cursed some of his friends and a few of his enemies and was well on its way to bedeviling him.

"Paris has always been and will always be awash in good wine. Even when Hadley and I were young and without means, we could afford proper wine," he remarked, somewhat out of context, to Mary, who sat at the dining room table with morning coffee and a few of the six newspapers that were delivered. She looked up but said nothing. She was there but was not listening and the references to Hadley made her even less interested.

"What's wrong, Kitten, cat got your tongue?" He asked

hoping for some kind of positive response. She had heard it too many times before and just looked at him. He didn't know whether she was sore at the Hadley reference or at the fact that he'd tied one on the night before... or both. Perhaps this was just the way it was going to be.

"Good morning," she said finally, more arctic than equatorial.

"Sore?"

"You could have behaved," she rebuked while René brought him coffee.

"I slept a little late, but I think I can get some words out if it's quiet."

"I think I'll go to Havana, there are some things I need to get to send back to Minnesota." She needed to get out.

"That would work. I'll see you for dinner then."

"Very well. But promise me you'll go easy tonight."

At his desk he read through his notes and realized there were some people running around Paris in the '20s that one needed a drink to endure and that Ford Madox Ford was one of them. He used to say that he drank to make others more interesting and Ford would have fallen into that category. He made Ernest feel uncomfortable, and the notes from 30 years ago made it clear that he suffered a lot of discomfort. Sitting there in Cuba so close to Christmas, he did have a touch of brotherly love but none of it was reserved for Ford Madox Ford. He had felt for a long time that Ford deserved a shot and now that he had passed away, he was a perfect target. He had actually blamed Ford for some of his own drinking. He always took the position that Ford was a very tough pill to swallow but would go down somewhat easier with a drink or two. Alice Toklas also required a chaser from time to time. Her face, like her nose, was long and narrow and when she cocked her head to one side, she looked—if you'd had a few—check that, if you'd had more than a few—like an uninspired Modigliani. Drinks for him in the '20s, he recalled, were beer and wine and whiskey, with an occasional diversion like the old standby among the Paris literati. It was made from wormwood, flavored with anise and was the favorite of a host of artists and authors—Picasso, Verlaine, Joyce, Modigliani, van Gogh, Proust, Crowley, Wilde and others not quite in his memory. The drink was absinthe and had come from Switzerland. For some it was hallucinogenic and it had been around since the late 1800's. As a general rule, green was not Ernest's favorite color in an alcohol and as far as it giving one visions, he felt he saw enough of those on whiskey. But he had tried it and liked it, after all, it was alcohol. He, and the others, were amused by the process, the ritual, as much as they were the drink. The drill went something like this: pour an ounce or two of absinthe into a glass. Then put a sugar cube on a filigreed absinthe spoon which rested on the rim of the glass and slowly pour cold water through the sugar into the absinthe.

Toulouse-Lautrec who more or less led the absinthe parade, to the point of having a glass tube put in his hollow cane to carry the stuff, passed away in 1901, 20 years before Ernest arrived. But one of Lautrec's legacies was a drink he called the earthquake—a diabolical mix of absinthe and cognac served in a wine goblet. Once at a party the guests were to give the name of the person they would enjoy having to dinner, Ernest had chosen Lautrec. He noted that although he was only 4'8" he was a giant of provocative paintings and prints. His fingerprints were all over 1920s Paris. There was a joke that his name, Henri Marie Raymond de Toulouse-Lautrec-Monfa, if turned on end was taller than he was. There was another alcoholic digression he remembered during one Paris summer. It went by the name of Pimms #1 and was a tan colored, gin-based liquor. For a few months there was no shortage of patrons drinking Pimms with lemonade and soda, garnished with, of all things, a cucumber. Sometimes the ladies would substitute mint or lime. Pimms was immensely popular for one summer, but since it was English, most Frenchmen eschewed the fad and it followed the sparrows out of town when the summer ended. He tasted it once and that was enough. But one of the Brit's who drank a lot of the stuff was Ford, who to Ernest would always be not much more than an unkempt mustache.

"Spring, at least then in Paris, was my favorite season," he told Hotch on a rainy afternoon in the living room. They each sat in the flower patterned armchairs hard by the bottle laden folding bar. "Later living in places like Key West and here, spring lost its significance. Here we have a 12 month growing season and the colors are on display nearly year-round. But spring in Paris was completely memorable. Cole Porter had it right, except his spring was a false spring, in a way, because he goes on to admit that he loves Paris in all the seasons. He loves Paris in the springtime but also every moment of the year, which is a feeling and conclusion to which I will always subscribe. Paris is good and true and is only there to love you if you let it." Hotch thought that his friend had spells when he was his old self, but they were getting scarce.

"People are the limiters of happiness except for the very few who are as good as spring itself," Ernest said again as he had 30 years ago. These chapters, he thought, are testament to that concept but curiously some of those whom he had cast in the limiters role, most of us would not have guessed, as they were kind to him before his ascendancy. "In my notes I described the goatherd I saw from our apartment window. It's a classic and very peculiar to its time. He was herding goats down the street, selling milk as he went. I wish one of my painting friends would have transferred the scene to canvas. The day I saw the goatherd, Hadley and I took a train trip to, and the bus back from, the steeplechase track at Enghien. On the ride over I would put her in the window seat and study her profile while watching Paris go by from left to right. I'm careful not to tell Hadley stories when Mary is about, but with you, Hotch, I can speak freely. I would kiss her lightly on the head. Her hair was strawberry and soft and would smell faintly of the baking Marie had accomplished at the apartment and the sandwiches she had organized. She would call me Tati and say things in a low voice. I would call her Cat. She was pretty to look at, with the afternoon sun on her face coming through the train window. And I would tell her she sweetened me and she would reach up and barely touch the scar on my forehead and whisper 'poor Tati'. Hotch had no trouble seeing his old friend drift back 30 years to Paris and to the first love of his life. Ernest was not here in Cuba sitting next to him, but rather was on the train outside of Paris, and he was writing out loud.

"We would ride in silence, taking in the streaming landscapes framed by the casement. She would reach for my hand and I'd give it. This wouldn't happen often, which made it a special afternoon. The hippodrome d'Enghien is on the edge of Paris—you've been there Hotch—then it had harness, flat and steeplechase. It's all of 100 acres and was a major excitement for us, especially on a sunny spring day. She would tell me she was very glad we decided in favor of the races and I would have to reassure her that it was okay that we were there and spending money even if we were not lucky. And then I can remember feeling a pang. I was stingy and I knew it, and at times like this I feel I was cheap and inconsiderate. She deserved better. I'm fairly certain sitting here with the lights steadily dimming that most of the women in my life deserved better. My philosophy in Paris was to do most things cheaply and that seemed to work. But days like that when my newspaper check may have been all but wiped clean, those days made memories and made Hadley lighthearted and vivid. I would tell her that I had been given a name or two, and she would perk up and ask me if I thought they were any good. And I would tell her I got them from Vincenzo, one of our friends from Milan whom she had met the day we went to the racecourse at San Siro where Agnes von Kurowsky and I had visited in 1918. And she would tell me she remembered and that she thought he was good and that maybe his names would be good, too. And I would tell her that Vincenzo could calculate an advantage at a racetrack. That particular day he indeed proved his worth, and we won and, when we would win, most times we would halve our bet, rather than doubling it, and Vincenzo would come through again. We called those champagne days because we would have a glass while waiting for the winning odds to post. Hadley, which was her way, would worry more about the animal than about our winnings. She would remind me how hard the horse would work and tell me that all we had to do was bet and we would get paid. And she would ask me how the horse got paid. When we won, Hadley would get one fourth of the earnings, I would take one fourth and half went to our racing account for the next time out. That was our system. If we really hit it hard, if the horse or horses would come home, we sometimes would treat ourselves to a meal at Prunier's, an upscale restaurant on the Avenue Victor Hugo—oysters, crab and a Sancerre sauvignon blanc from the menu. After that we would take a satisfying walk home in the dark with the monuments lit. There was a story that Miss Stein had told us about the monuments in Paris and one in Milan that were supposedly in a direct line. The Arc du Carrousel, built to commemorate Napoleon's victories. The Arc de Triomphe, honoring the dead from the revolution and Napoleonic wars as well as the Unknown Soldier from World War I, and the obelisk in the Place de la Concorde are supposedly in a direct line with the Arch of Peace in Milan, a distance of some 500 miles.

"In my notes Miss Stein's theory that these monuments connect France to Italy is compared to St. Bernard pass that at over 8000 feet connects Switzerland to Italy and where Hadley and I and Chink did part of the trek on foot when we were traveling the 50 odd miles from Martigny to Aosta.

"Chink was Major General Eric Edward Dorman-Smith, who, for a reason I cannot remember, changed his surname to Dorman O'Gowan. He fought in World War 1 and later he would fight in World War II. He was bright and decorated and saw much action. His nickname resulted from his supposed resemblance to the Chinkara antelope which was the mascot of his regiment. I met Chink in Italy in 1918 and then in Paris in 1922 when we went on this memorable trip to Montreux, Switzerland to fish and climb mountains. On our way to Milan, Hadley and I and Chink crossed the St. Bernard Pass on foot, which sounds like, and was, a decision fueled by wine, schnapps and thin mountain air. I also found Jim Gamble's name in a journal, but someone, probably me, had spilled something on those pages so the story remains a mystery. All I could read from the washed out writing was that Gamble had told a story involving wisteria or hysteria… not much to go on. I do remember that Jim Gamble was my c.o. in the ambulance corps and a great pal who took care of me when I was laid up in Italy in July, 1918. I also remember that he was from Pennsylvania and that I called him Chief.

"Chink and I would discuss how military orders and directions should be like prose writing. They both should be minimalistic, with simple grammar, austere wording and as unvarnished as possible. They should be short, easy to understand, declarative sentences with few adjectives to get in the way. Ezra would have completely agreed. His goal was to use as few words as possible and I think he was the cause of a tale I told to win a bet that I could use six words to tell a story. 'For sale: baby shoes never worn.' I think I'd also seen something similar years before...something like 'baby carriage for sale, never used'."

And so they sat there, the brilliant but fading literary star and his friend Hotch, while Ernest, with little or no transition, talked him abruptly back to Paris and the Louvre and the Seine and then magically back to Switzerland and trout and white wine and looking out on the Dents du Midi, the seven summits in the Chablais Alps, which are called the "Teeth of Noon", as they resemble teeth rising out of a jawbone. Then Ernest, now prone to confusion, quickly led his friend, once again, back to Paris. Sometimes he was slow, sometimes he moved at top speed. But Hotch had the feeling that Ernest couldn't tell the difference.

"So we went again to Michaud's, which was an extravagant excitement. I always hoped to see Joyce there. He, Nora, Giorgio and Lucia all ate there from time to time, conversing in Italian and looking educated and at ease. Giorgio wore the same style wire rims as his father. Imagine Hotch, all those celebrities in one city at the same time, a real syzygy, all the stars lined up along the Seine. I can actually remember Hadley slept well that night with the moon kissing her face, just as the sun had done earlier on the train and when she slept on my coat on the grass at the racetrack."

Once again Ernest seemed wrapped around the concept of hunger. It seemed to be the hunger of being poor—whether for food or fun or paintings or anything else. It was hunger and it ate at him. The word hunger appeared in the notebooks as many times as the word literature. He remembered sleepless nights on their good mattress in their fire-placed bedroom in the blue-collar neighborhood in Paris. Some nights before he rose to spend what would be an inordinate amount of time at the window, he would kiss Hadley's hair in the moonlight. Over the years he would dream about those kisses in the moonlight and then one night 30 years ago he wrote the kind of sentence that made him famous… "But Paris was a very old city and we were young and nothing was simple there, not even poverty, nor sudden money, nor the moonlight, nor right and wrong, nor the breathing of someone who lay beside you in the moonlight."

THE RACES

Some days here in Cuba he missed the cool, soft air of Idaho, the soughing of the pines, the mountains rising, the sad turning of the leaves and the smell of wood fires in the fireplace or even just the scent of the fireplace, alone, when the fire had died. The days would be shorter and sometimes it would be a blessing. He grew tired much earlier now while watching hints that the Idaho winter was in the vicinity. He would leave before it came, mostly for his health. He would come back to Cuba where the weather was more welcoming and easier on his many maladies, but winter had always been an important part of his past. He had been skiing since he and Hadley learned in Schruns, in the Montafon valley, where they would stay from Thanksgiving to Easter. Now it was as if winter didn't exist and he missed it. His father had taught him all the outdoor pursuits of winter back in Michigan and he was sad for their absence. Cuba was excellent—he had lived here longer than anywhere—but that wasn't to say he didn't miss the others: Africa, Spain, Italy, Key West, Canada, France, England, Chicago, Idaho, Michigan and others and maybe even, on a desperate afternoon, Oak Park.

It was early morning just past 6:30. It was time to work, time to write. His output now was between 400 and 700 words a day. But he knew he was slowing. He wrote in longhand and he typed but neither was as easy as it once was. He had scanned one of the half dozen newspapers he and Mary received every day. He had a guest coming. An editor of a stateside magazine here to do an interview. The gentleman had wanted to stay longer, but Ernest cut it to one day. The plan was to take him out on the *Pilar*—put the rods in, drink a little, talk about the sea, have a little lunch and offer him some cigars. Gregorio would point out any breachers or birds and the dark edge of the Gulfstream. The birds would show them the fish and maybe the interviewer would ask some questions about the Gulf and Ernest would tell him that the sea was the last free place.

Reading through the yellowed Ritz notebooks, he realized that fishing in Cuba had replaced horse racing in Paris. It was a good trade, a healthier trade—and one that certainly required more physical skill. But racing was an essential entertainment of his in the '20s and assuredly deserved a place in the Paris book. So throughout the day, which was not a normal day, he thought about how to organize a chapter around horse racing.

Racing became the default entertainment of the Paris Hemingway's. It was an afternoon amusement, scheduled after his morning of writing. It was popular with both of them, the splendid animals and the thrill of the earth-jarring race, all gilded by the bet.

"It was not like all the other recreations we enjoyed, with our favorite friends from assorted places," he said later in the afternoon to Mary, Hotch and Gregorio, his friend for 32 years and after whom he had named one of his sons. Gregorio had also saved Greg's life by shooting a shark and had been to a few races himself out at Oriental Park in Marianao, Havana.

"It wasn't really the race course or even the running. It was the chance, the speculation, the potential hazard of the wager. It was the risk, not the run, but we called it racing because it felt better in the ear. Racing was an exacting, exhausting accomplice; always pressing, always wearing, rarely joyful or forgiving. It was the chaperone with his hand in your pocket, as false as some springs. To make it pay would take all of one's energy and time. To misquote Miss Stein, one would have to not spend money on clothes, to buy racing tickets. To quote me, one would have to forsake almost everything else."

Eventually he left Hadley behind; and the trips to the track, instead of a lazy afternoon, sunlit diversion, became astringent and desperate. He doubled his odds, by working both Enghien and Auteuil. He did not double his winnings.

"It was a job with many tasks and really not enough time

to complete them; watching the race, studying each horse, monitoring the prices and the developing odds, and then, over time, you would learn the good stables—and who was reliable for a name now and then. But it was too much to do for one man; and despite the fascination and the beauty of a good race with clean and fine horses, over time you would glimpse the underbelly of the sport and one afternoon it occurred. I knew things I did not want to know. I knew too much. This is when the better part of me, not the reckless or the foolhardy me, but the astute and more judicious part, warned me to leave it behind. So I left it behind. I put the racing money into our joint account and left the racing to others. And when Mike, a good friend and I had lunch, I found out that he had also quit the races and asked his reason. His answer was worthy of a frame, 'anything you bet on to get a kick, isn't worth seeing'."

Mike was a nickname he gave Thomas Ward, a Canadian born Paris banker. He was a good friend and very protective of Ernest and evidently once served up a punch in the nose to a barfly who he thought disparaged his friend.

"Although I gave up horses, Mike who had done the same, suggested I go to the bicycle races with him. It became an important diversion. There were no horses to manipulate and it was fast and sometimes you would hold your breath when it was dangerous. At first I was content to bet on myself and my morning writing, but later I disappeared into cycling. I learned it like I learned to fish. I plunged into it like the riders themselves plunged after climbing on the high banked wood track. Hadley and I would go to six day bicycle races. We would take supper and a thermos and sit on cushions. Sometimes we would stay all night with our pillows and blankets. I could hear music in the hum of the tires. I understood drafting and strategy and aerodynamics and top speeds and men racing against time and men racing against men and I came to know the 'Cherry Brandy Champ' whose hand I shook at the outdoor track at Montrouge. He was the Belgian champion known as 'the Sioux' because of his Native American looks who sucked cherry brandy from a rubber bottle, covered by his racing shirt, via a rubber tube. In all of the cafés I visited, that I never bothered to count by the way, I never saw or heard of such a delivery system. But then I never drank much cherry brandy either. But from the comedy of the Sioux, I went to the tragedy of Ganay who broke his skull on the cement track near Auteuil. I was there, saw his fall and heard his fall and was haunted by his fall. I remembered it as a slow motion, grotesque, real life version of Humpty Dumpty. "

Gustave Ganay was a French cyclist who died from a horrific fall at the *Parc des Princes*, so named for the land on which it was built, which had been a hunting forest used by French royals. He died on Monday, August 23, 1926 from head wounds suffered when he fell from his bike onto a cement track. Victor Linhert was another Belgian cycling champ Ernest enjoyed. He won his first race at 14, fought in the war and then became a professional cyclist winning 15 national championships. Ernest always tipped his hat to bravery and prowess.

He fell off the betting wagon and went back to horse racing when he met Evan Shipman who had grown up around horses and handicapped professionally. The two would take frequent trips to both tracks and Ernest's winning percentage increased. Hemingway taught Shipman to fish, Shipman taught him to handicap horses. Shipman had learned the art of handicapping in the betting tents of the racing circuit. Ernest said that one of his favorite things to do was to sit with Evan and learn the form and then try to pick winners in the blue smoky afternoons and then go out and play them at Auteuil and Enghien. One day Shipman went to the track and lost 'all his jack' betting. He had to meet his sister so, penniless, he jumped a train. A railway policeman found him and was going to arrest him and give him 60 days, until they started talking and the officer discovered what a likable soul Shipman was. He wound up buying Shipman a meal instead of arresting him.

APPETITES

In May 1959, Ernest and Mary arrived in Spain aboard the S.S. Constitution. Since 1939, the end of the Spanish Civil War where he had covered the hostilities with Martha Gellhorn, he had only returned to Spain for short stays, mostly to witness bullfights. The Spanish Civil War had started when Franco led a revolt, which started in Morocco and then spread to the Spanish mainland, against the democratically elected Republican government. Ernest and other artists and writers supported the loyalists who opposed Franco. With Franco's victory in 1939, a 40 year dictatorship began in Spain. This war had been important to Ernest and he vowed not to return to Spain until those he knew were released from Franco's prisons.

On this 1959 trip he stayed in Ronda, a breathtaking city perched on a 300-foot cliff. Ronda was also home to the world's largest bullring. Although he and Mary usually stayed in hotels for privacy, this time they stayed at the mansion, *La Consula,* owned by American's Ann and Bill Davis, the brother-in-law of literary critic Cyril Connolly. The wealthy expats opened their home to the Hemingway's and a young Irish journalist, Valerie Danby-Smith, who had been sent to interview the aging author.

The Davis's mansion, with a 60 foot pool and very white marble, furniture and walls, on which hung significant art, was the site of Ernest's two day 60th birthday party that Jay Gatsby would have envied. It had about everything you could think of for a party including Lauren Bacall and a shooting booth. Although he had the Paris book with him, most of his writing on this trip centered on bullfighting and eventually led to *The Dangerous Summer* published in June 1985. Bullfighting was a devotion for Ernest. Not so much for Mary but she accompanied him to the *plazas de toros*. Back in Idaho when he finally touched the sun, there were tickets on his dresser for the bullfights in Pamplona that were to take place the following week. His first trip to Spain had been in 1922 to Pamplona for the running of the bulls. The *Sun Also Rises* had its basis in his third trip in 1924. In 1937 when he had come to Spain to cover the Spanish Civil War for a newspaper, Martha Gellhorn, whom he had met in Key West, joined him in Madrid. He wrote the *Fifth Column* there and remarked that the nights never ended in Madrid and that no one goes to bed there until they have killed the night. Typically plans in Madrid were made to meet people after midnight. In July 1960 his legendary 60th birthday party went from noon on the 21st to noon on the 22nd.

While in Spain he did take time to read through some of the transcriptions Nita had typed. It was early morning and he set on the pillared veranda of *La Consula* reading his reformed 30-year-old notes and vignettes. From a 1959 vantage point, a 60-year-old's vantage point, reading through the sketches, made so long ago in a life and time that no longer existed and reflecting on what he had accomplished, it occurred to him that he was writing his own legend. Even the more modest part of him, admittedly a small and overshadowed part, was impressed that he had been famous at 25. But the tired, diseased and unsteady part of him realized that his 60th birthday party might have been his last hurrah, his last international adventure. There had been many of those, but now they would most likely be reduced to cruises on the *Pilar,* when he returned to Cuba. Nonetheless the old soldier, wounded, stitched up, wounded again permanently, soldiered on and began organizing another chapter. He had mentioned to several of his friends that he did not look good in twilight—but now, at least for this short time it was dawn and it was bright and pleasant and he felt better. Twilight, however, was not far away.

"Sitting here in the beauty of the Davis mansion, in Ronda, a gem of a place running along a 500 foot gorge, it is challenging to remember the circumstances that caused me to write about the hunger that was such an important discipline to me when I was young and poor in Paris. However staying here, with all the wealth and opulence and other trappings of prosperity, might be just the prism through which to view the imposed discipline of hunger. Knut Hemsun wrote an entire book about it. What the hell, I'll give it a try. Good writing grows out of confidence and hunger. There is really nothing to writing—just sit down at a typewriter and bleed or as Blaise Cendrars saw it, just sit down and burst into flames.

In the 1920s notebooks, hunger was a constant theme and at times he thought it might be too constant. The young artist complained of hunger but endured it and used it as a discipline, a rule of order around which he organized his life. In the first schoolboy notebook he opened were notes on hunger and how the *gastronomique* scents of Paris make you hungry even when you're not. So to dispatch these temptations, he would pick places to go like the Luxembourg Gardens or Museum where there were no food scents, no sidewalk cafés with delights of food and drink to tempt him, to make him hungry.

"Back then hunger in the stomach seemed to help me understand some paintings and some painters and then I would think of the different ways there are to be hungry. In fact I thought hunger should be a required course, because there is a lot to learn from hunger. The café sketches in the notebooks contain drawings and walking instructions to avoid restaurants and their siren-like lure. I used to focus on benches and trees and fountains and statues and shops selling objects other than food. I would try to avoid temptation with the hope that my hunger would abate or at least not be worsened. I remember Bertolt Brecht wrote to me once that hungry men reach for books. Sometimes I reach for them to keep my mind from picturing, and my stomach from calling, for food. The empty stomach is an ungrateful beast, it is always on the offensive for more and it is not a good confidant or counselor—but it can teach you self-control and willpower. It is the bedfellow of abstinence and moderation. I wrote back there in Paris that I was trying not to tease my stomach, trying not to arouse my hunger but I was desperately looking for an excuse to do it and finally Sylvia Beach gave me one. I can remember her telling me I was too thin—hard to imagine now. I have it more than once in the notes that she kept asking me if I was eating enough and repeated her offer for Hadley and me to have dinner at her home with Adrienne. Her plans were to invite us to a dinner with Paul Fargue and Valery Larbaud, two writers that I had not yet met but wanted to. Paul was a French poet and essayist and a friend to Rilke and the French composer Ravel. He had also introduced Proust to James Joyce. Larbaud was a French author, translator and was the first critic to evaluate Joyce's *Ulysses*. Both would make excellent dinner partners for a young writer and his wife. Sylvia was doing what she did best. She put people together. It was what I needed. She treated me well and now was going to feed me. She was a good friend. She held mail for me at the library. I trusted her with payments that I was receiving for stories I was able to publish. It saved me worrying, having a person like Sylvia taking care of things for me.

"One of the sketches I found in a notebook centered on Sylvia giving me a letter from Hermann von Wedderkop, a German author and editor of a German art magazine in which I was lucky enough to publish, in the fall of 1924, a poem called *The Lady Poets With Footnotes*. It was about six lady poets who everyone knew and I did not treat them respectfully. A lot of people called it mean-spirited. Hadley called it nasty. The poem was a satire. It poked some not-so-funny fun at the girls. When I wrote it all the ladies were very much alive and though Hadley and I were not a household of means, I wanted to protect what we had; therefore the ladies were nameless. Now it's 1957 and all but one are no longer with us, so I could list the five who are not: Edna St. Vincent Millay, Aline Kilmer, Sara Teasdale, Lola Ridge and Amy Lowell but not Zoe Akins who still lives and who showed me a thing or two. Since I wrote about her, she has won a Pulitzer for dramatizing Edith Wharton's 'Old Maid' and wrote a lot of successful movies. But I think I shall leave all of this out of the Paris book, if for no other reason than to honor Hadley.

As for honoring Hadley, I should really organize a chapter apologizing to her. It would be an honest and sincere gesture, but I would never get it past the war department ... so it will be left out of this book.

But back to the lady poets, Miss Stein would have punched me, Hadley wanted to—but it was Fr.600 and my work was not selling well yet. The only other publication I was having any luck with at all was in Germany also. Then Sylvia, always trying to find a way to help, asked me about Ford Madox Ford and the *Transatlantic Review*. I walked her through his pay scale and calculated that selling him stories at Fr.30 a page, I could maybe make in a year, what Wedderkop had given me for a one-page slightly off-color poem. With Ford I would have been perpetually hungry and not very happy. Years later a Spanish novelist, his first name is Carlos but I can't remember his surname, which at one time I knew as well as my own, coined a phrase that fit me perfectly in the early '20s. 'Paris is the only city in the world where starving to death is still considered an art.' Sylvia made a big deal out of making me promise her that I would eat enough, which I did. But these were uncertain times for me. I had quit journalism and was not making much money selling a poem here or a short story there. The checks from the Toronto Star had stopped. We still had Hadley's $3000 a year inheritance, but some questionable investments had reduced that. We were far from prosperous or even independent.

Sitting here reading and writing about Hadley raises an issue I'd rather avoid if I could, but I can't. Mary and I have been married since 1946, but she still reacts whenever I mention any of the other wives—especially Hadley and especially now as we are not doing well together. Like me, I think she knows that maybe my first wife, deep down, was my favorite.

"So although we were far from prosperous, in fact we were poor, I still had some friends at the time who would loan me money. I can remember, about this time—which surprises even me—going to one of my favorite places for food and drink. It was a German café called Lipp's, a brasserie on the Boulevard Saint-Germain where Camus and Chagall frequented, dining on potato laden fare and stout beer. After Sylvia and I had been talking about the Germans and the poem I had sold them, it got me to thinking about German food and before I knew it I was sitting in Lipp's. It had become one of my favorites with its array of sausages, potatoes and stout ales. It was also special, I think, because I had an epiphany of sorts while sitting there. I was worried about making enough money to support my wife and son. But Edward O'Brien, God bless him, had given me courage when he not only published *My Old Man* but dedicated the anthology to me. It couldn't have come at a better time. *My Old Man* was one of only two pieces that hadn't gone missing when the valise disappeared at the Gare de Lyon. I was extremely grateful to Mr. O'Brien for publishing the piece even though he misspelled my last name, something Scott Fitzgerald did for two years. The only reason *My Old Man* survived was because an editor had refused it and sent it back to me and it had not arrived before Hadley packed up the valise to go to Switzerland. The other piece that had survived was *Up in Michigan*. The reason I still had that story was because Miss Stein had told me, because of its subject matter, it was unpublishable. Finally my morale matched my hunger. My spirit was hopeful. I was more resolute and maybe the gap was closing somewhat between the dream and the reality.

"Edward O'Brien had begun editing a short story anthology in 1915. He sought out what he considered the best contemporary authors and I was flattered that he had included me and had honored me with the dedication. He expressed confidence in me and helped me publish my own short story collection *In Our Time* in 1925. I had actually written two sketches about this in the Paris notebooks. I was proud of myself at the time, things were starting to turn the corner. My anthology contained six prose sketches Ezra Pound had commissioned for the 1923 edition of *The Little Review* which Ezra helped to create. It became famous for the serialization of Joyce's *Ulysses*. I had written 14 short stories which were included.

"As a result of my training under Pete Wellington at the Kansas City Star and advice from my literary friends in Paris at the time, my short stories then were minimalist—void of anything complex. I tried for a clear and direct style. The journalism showed through. Since then it has been described as short, direct, clipped, cablese—and any number of adjectives indicating the simple, declarative, one thought sentences. Many other writers at the time were going the other way, Joyce being the extreme example, but I was aiming for straightforward, uncomplicated, plain and quiet. I wanted sentences to be manageable, uninvolved and not difficult or troublesome. I spent a lot of time in Paris thinking about writing stories that were refused and what it would take to change that.

Then came December 3, 1922 and the lost valise that held most of my work to date. That was a punch in the gut. I had even gone back to Paris from Switzerland to search for the carbons and found that they also had been lost. Hadley had been sick with worry. I remember patting her on the head and then holding her close when the patting didn't chase the dread. But that loss was over now and my military friends, Chink and Smitty, both had told me in different ways at different times and with different examples, never to discuss casualties. It was a great lesson, but a hard lesson to accept. It is in my notes that I said aloud that it was okay for me to lose those stories and that I would be okay. I would write more and the Edward O'Briens and the Wudderkops of the world would publish them, and Sylvia and Ezra and others would help me find other publishers to take them.

"Two of the schoolboy notebooks that were given back to me at Charlie Ritz's office contained slightly different explanations of what came to be known as the iceberg theory. Basically it trades on the fact that most of an iceberg is below the surface, and so it could be with a story or a poem or any writing for that matter. In the journals I use *Out of Season* as an example. I had omitted the ending which was a suicide. And I can remember in Paris thinking about my father and Hadley's father, James Richardson, and Pascin who had all killed themselves. So the biggest thing in *Out of Season* was the suicide, and by omitting it, I brought even more attention to it. So the iceberg theory, or the theory of omission as I called it in one of the journals, was that the author could omit anything and the exclusion would strengthen the story by focusing more attention on the unseen or undescribed event. Readers would feel more than they understood, would know more than they were reading. There is one sketch in the books where I'm explaining it to Ezra and I tell him that it made sense, this omission, because if the reader can't quite see it, it makes him anticipate what is left out, makes him envision it, maybe even create a little on his own. He is apt to foresee, imagine and maybe even conjure up the missing piece. I can leave it out, and he can read it in. Read it in his mind's eye. Like they do with paintings. The reader will see things in the stories, as the viewer does in artwork.

"I've said this before, I think, it's getting so I don't remember well at all but it's amazing as I sit here reading these sketches in my own handwriting, how many times I talk about hunger. I over did it. It's as if hunger punctuated everything. In this one sketch I talk about hunger-thinking. I had told Sylvia that hunger-thinking had never led me to anything good. Hunger was a discipline but if you were too hungry it was not favorable. Like Gandhi said, 'there are people so hungry that God himself could not appear to them except in the form of bread.' My father told me once that when all you have is a hammer, everything starts to look like a nail. If all you think about is hunger, your stories are going to read like potatoes and beer. I had said that a hungry man is a good observer, he is alert, is expectant—and I believe that. And there are other kind of hungers that are useful. For example when you are responsible for your own well-being and that of your family, you'll have a hunger to accomplish and that will usually drive you to good things. It is a clear, specific appetite to succeed that is valuable. In my notes I found a rather sophomoric sentence but it nevertheless carried the message. Hunger is an unalloyed, explicit eagerness to achieve, a fascination with triumph. Where the hell is the short, direct, clipped journalism style in that?

"There's another example of hunger in the notebooks that I found interesting. I remembered one of the waiters at the Café Select. He had been born with a cleft palate and as a result his speech was not clear, and he was rather difficult to understand. The great thing was he didn't let it bother him, so it didn't bother others. He worked very hard on his speech. He had a hunger to improve, and he did and he was proud and he should've been. We all celebrated his new speech. Without these journals I would've never remembered that waiter with courage.

"I had spent a good deal of time in the cafés applying the hunger principle to writing, saying things like hunger is a good discipline and like gambling is a demanding partner. George Eliot had written and I had read that there are certain things we have to have to be beautiful and good and that we should hunger after them. Just wanting to write something good and true is not enough, you have to hunger for it. And I did. I remember the time in Paris when I knew that the next thing I had to write was a novel and I hungered for it, a lot. Scott had written one and I knew I had to. And I remember telling Hadley that I had to do this and she said, 'Yes Tati, you are ready for it and it is ready for you' and she put her hand to my cheek. It was just the right thing to do. Her timing was always remarkable. Sometimes I really do miss her. At any rate I told her then that I knew I could do it, I would just have to start by writing longer stories and then joining them like the cars on the train. There was a novel in the valise that went missing so I knew I could do it. I had done it before. But I was not going to write it just to eat regularly and well. From very early on I had a problem with that concept. It doesn't make as much sense to me now sitting here in Cuba, but it did then. I had criticized Scott for writing for money. I should've known that it was not a misdemeanor to feed yourself and your family with your pen or your brush. A lot of us were poor back then and were trying to make a living by doing what we did best, whether it was writing or painting or editing or publishing.

"I'm afraid with all the things that are going wrong with me that I'm not as good at organizing or writing, or anything else for that matter, as I used to be. When I read through the journals instead of pulling out all the information on one topic, I'm skipping around and I hope it won't be too much of a distraction. For example now I find myself back at Lipp's, knee-deep in potatoes and sausage and bread and clear, cold beer. Good for Lipp's. Good for German food. They fought two bad wars but they made hearty food.

"In those days I had a habit of taking coffee at a café different from where we had eaten. Hadley often thought it was an unnecessary exercise when we were seated and warm and the food was just what it should be at the first café. But the afternoon I sketched in the notebooks took place at *Deux Magots* or "Two Macaques" which describe the large mandarin statues decorating the interior. A lot of the usual suspects ate there including Picasso, Brecht and later Camus. Often when my stomach was full, the pad and pencil came out and I would look around for something that I liked and knew something about. Often the afternoon sun would shaft through the Café windows at odd angles and expose the dust mites that danced and swirled behind the waiters as they moved quickly and expertly between tables. I would write about war, about coming back from the war but sometimes I wouldn't mention the war—the iceberg. I had told Scott and others that every writer should go through at least one war. Of course I had been through more than one and was therefore loaded for bear; and sadly as I see it now, lorded it over those who hadn't seen a war, never mind that I was never a combatant."

Peers in the expat community who had not gone to war; but who instead had the advantage of a formal, often Ivy League, education may not have had the experience that Ernest deemed necessary to good writing, but did have a certain discipline and temperance that was absent in his makeup. He had a volatile temper, suffered from jealousy and was a sore loser. Add to this the Gerald Murphys of the world with unlimited wealth and stunning wives and there was a lot more to envy; and whether he ever suspected or not, he took out his frustrations on them, especially if he had taken a run at their wives and been rebuffed, as in the case of Sarah Murphy. Later Gerald Murphy Would say, "*A Moveable Feast* is such a mean book but so well written."

FORD MADOX FORD & ALEISTER CROWLEY

This chapter had been worked on in both Spain and Cuba. It was cobbled together from several sources pulled from the trunks including some letters and newspaper clips.

"If I had to pick one favorite café in the Paris of the '20s it would be the *Closerie des Lilas* which had been on the Boulevard Montparnasse since 1847. The Lilas was close to our second apartment above the saw mill at 113 rue Notre-Dame des Champs. Inside in the winter where it was warm, outside in the garden in summer where it was cooler, the notebooks and pencil spent time in this garden of lilacs, not far from my newly made friend Mike Ney. I considered it 'my café'.

"Hadley and I had moved in above the saw mill, nice enough place but a little noisy when the blade was running. The strong clean scent of the wood made up for most of the noise. Evidently the former tenant had been an American named Gorham Munson and for the first few weeks, some surprised faces appeared at our open door asking if Gorham were there. One of those faces belonged to Evan Shipman who turned out to be a swell human being and one of my best friends. I planned to write a chapter about him and include it in the Paris book. We'll see how my plan works out.

"Jean, a waiter at the Lilas, was partial to Evan and me. Jean had a garden that he worked on weekends and would bring us tomatoes, carrots, and onions. He enjoyed this bit of commerce as did we. There were certain patrons of the upscale Dome and Rotonde cafés who didn't visit the Lilas because there was no one there they knew and no one would have stared at them if they came. There were those who thought I went to some cafés for the same reason— perhaps I did. There was one patron at the Lilas who I would've enjoyed meeting but never did. His name was Paul Fort and I had never seen him or ever read any of his work, but the waiters said he spent afternoons from time to time in the Lilas.

Fort was a legitimate child prodigy who founded a theater when he was 18 years old. He was a poet and playwright. Verlaine called him the Prince of Poets and his most famous poem was *La Ronde*—a plea for world friendship, certainly an admirable goal. I did see Blaise Cendrars there and I remember this very well because Blaise was very difficult to miss or forget. Blaise had lost his right arm fighting for the French Foreign Legion. His real name was Frédéric-Louis Sauser but he adopted the pen name Blaise Cendrars which was a combination of Latin and French words for blaze, cinders and art. The name symbolizes writing as burning up and then rising from the ashes. He was a Swiss novelist and the first exponent of modernism in European poetry. I remember at the time that Ezra thought this was a huge deal and greatly admired Cendrars, who was a friend of Apollinaire and a favorite of Miss Stein and answered to 'the left-handed poet'. I used to sit in the Lilas and watch him closely. He was as good with just one arm as I was with two. After a while I felt that I was disadvantaged by having two arms. He had been through much, living in Switzerland, Germany, Russia and especially at the front at Somme in 1916 where he lost his arm. He would describe the war as if he were a reporter, allowing you to picture the battle at Somme and sense how deadly it was when the Allies tried to break through the 25 mile long German front along the river. He certainly could tell a story. With his empty right sleeve, battle ribbons and his asymmetrical face, Cendrars looked the consummate warrior. I respected him for what he'd done with his rifle and his pen.

Understandably he drank like a legionnaire and the drink nourished his stories which seemed to pullulate with each glass. I had asked him how it was with just one arm, after drinking a liter myself, 'Better than none—not as good as two'. I remember being annoyed at myself for asking. He spoke with experience and passion and as if from a vantage point above—but at the same time he was pragmatic, plain spoken and unassuming. I had written in the sketch about him that some patrons thought he might be showing off his missing arm but perhaps it might just have been the iceberg theory at work. It might have been his arm's absence that made it so loud and nothing he intended at all. I liked the old soldier in him.

Other soldiers came in, in those days Paris was full of soldiers, some, like Blaise, mere sketches of themselves. The older men, dingy and bleak, with their colorful miniature hearts on their chests, if not their sleeves, in the form of battle ribbons from the Great War. They were not there to be seen by anybody and I would sit among them and drink and write. There were times when I wanted to say something to them, something honorable, something fair and proper in French; but I never did—there were so many.

"One of the journals, as I think I mentioned earlier, had something spilled on it making the writing difficult to decipher. On one page about Ford Madox Ford, however the liquid might've been tears of boredom. One night, musing over a drink I looked up and there was Ford Hermann Hueffer, who now called himself Ford Madox Ford because his real name sounded too German for these war times. Ford was an English writer who edited the *Transatlantic Review* and the *English Review* to help young writers get a start in publishing. He had written one very good book, *The Good Soldier* for which I really never forgave him. I thought the book was far too good to have been written by a man for whom I had such little respect. It didn't add up. He was a mouth breathing, overweight beer container with a mottled, unsanitary mustache. I always thought he would make a splendid missing person. He asked me if he could sit with me, he might as well have asked me if he could stick his finger in my eye. Ford could be a real pain in the ass and he didn't smell all that outstanding either. He sat there and stared out from his inflated face with those vacuous eyes. Mostly he and I would argue and one night we started arguing like we'd been doing lately, but I relented and finally offered him a drink.

Jean, a really good and decent waiter at the Lilas, took the order and Ford immediately lapsed into his ass mode by first ordering a glass of black currant wine and then after Jean had written that down, changing his order to brandy and water. Remember, these drinks were on me and when Jean returned with the brandy, Ford with a good deal of arrogance, scolded Jean and told him he had gotten it all wrong, that he had ordered wine. Everybody there, including the ass, knew that he had changed his order to brandy but Jean of course took the blame that wasn't his. I drank the brandy and Ford slurped his black currant wine transferring to his mustache more than its share.

"I dodged Ford when I could and bypassed his gaze when I couldn't. Looking at him, especially directly, was something I would go to great lengths to escape. This day, I recount in my notes, he accused me of being glum which depressed me even more than usual, and then he argued with me about it. He argued about everything. He told me to get out more, I wanted to tell him that's exactly what I wanted to do, thanks to his intrusion. And then in truly Ford Hermann Hueffer, turned Ford Madox Ford, fashion he kept it up and went on about me getting out more. I told him that if I got out anymore I wouldn't have to pay rent at my apartment. He wanted me to join him at the *bal musette* which was right below where I used to live. The *bal musette* was a small, working class dance hall with a bar and an accordion band. It was fun for Hadley, as she liked to dance. She used to tell me I was a good dancer but I wasn't. I told everyone that the mortar fragments had left my legs graceless, but in all honesty I wasn't all that good before the mortar. I did lose some mobility when I lost the illusion that getting a war wound wouldn't happen to me. But she insisted I was still a good dancer because I was tall and her head fit well on my shoulder and my shoulder was steady and made her feel safe. Hadley was so damn good that way. I would tell her that I would always try to make her feel safe and calm and she would ask me if I promised and I would say in French that yes I promised.

"Ford made a very big deal about telling me where the party was going to be and he kept on about me not knowing where it was going to be held, even after I told him I had lived right above it. Even after I repeated that I knew where the damn place was, he kept on telling me how to get there. I would tell him I knew where it was and he would give me more directions. What the hell was wrong with the guy? I began to think that keeping him alive was a waste of breath. And then, as if he had not confused the conversation enough, he told Jean he had made another mistake with the drinks. Again it was cassis versus brandy. He was again, of course, dead ass wrong—a state with which I'm sure he was intimately familiar. I told Jean I would again take the brandy and let the poor son of a bitch sitting and smelling and spitting next to me have the wine. So Ford Madox Hueffer had his unordered cassis as I was thinking of ways to put some real estate between the two of us.

"And then it happened. A rather thin, forlorn, angular man passed outside in front of the window. He was with a tall dramatic woman. It was not meant to be a grand stroll although the two characters were so striking that it appeared that way. The man glanced at us on his way by and Ford gets all excited and asks me if I saw the way he cut the man. Cutting was the 1920s description of snubbing someone, so Ford was asking me if I saw the way he had shot the man a disparaging look, as if somehow it could diminish the other person, weaken or reduce him. The fact was that Ford's sentence had bankrupted him. It was Ford who had been cheapened by the episode. But he was quick to tell me that he had just snubbed Belloc. Hilaire Belloc, I had learned from Miss Stein, was an Anglo—French writer. He was a very large man, powerfully built—no one would have used the words thin or angular to describe him. He was the brother of Marie Belloc Lowndes—a favorite of Gertrude's. For some reason she liked his quote about there falls no shadow where there shines no sun. Ford, in a revealing display of self-doubt, asked me if he, in fact, had cut Belloc or not. Did I cut him? Did I? The correct answer to that was no. I did not know Belloc and didn't even think the man in the cape on the sidewalk had noticed us. I would've liked to have met Belloc—those kinds of contacts were one of the reasons my attendance at the Lilas was so regular. Meeting Belloc would have mitigated the unpalatable taste left by Ford and his boorish attitude. To me Ford's wanting personal hygiene was eclipsed only by his vulgar demeanor.

He was coarse and crude and not very wondrous to be around.

"On more than one occasion I came close to raking Ford's outsize posterior over the coals. Hadley would not have approved in the least and of course she would, once again, be correct. But Ford had earned his bona fides as a certified pain in the ass and was about to show that he didn't know that same ass from much else. Ford Madox was, in fact, about a chapter and a half behind. But Ezra had told me to play nice, that Ford had been through a domestic nightmare and that, after all was said and done, he was a good writer. Now I loved Ezra and I knew he was straight and true when he wasn't mad and crazed and I trusted his judgment, so for Ezra's sake I endured—even though Ford was altogether unpleasant to be with and sat so close to me I thought I had two profiles.

"This whole business about cutting escaped me. It wasn't in my daily vocabulary and I wasn't exactly sure what it entailed. For some reason I thought I'd heard about it happening in one of Ouida's novels, though I had never read one so someone must've told me. Her real name was Maria Rame. She was an English novelist who got her nickname from her own juvenile mispronunciation of Louise. Perhaps her parents should've considered speech therapy. But she was not boring in the least. She was a bit of an extremist who took a hotel room, wrote in bed by candle light surrounded by purple everything and held court with the likes of Oscar Wilde, Swinburne, Robert Browning and Wilkie Collins. Now that's a strange bedroom full. She wasn't a real head turner, inasmuch as she looked like a two-armed, female version of Blaise Cendrars and had a tongue not unlike a razor. At one time she owned as many as 30 dogs. Now I'm a cat person and I generally like pets but 30 dogs—can't see it.

"Anyway things got at least tolerable with Ford when the two of us played a made up game involving who in history were gentlemen and who were not. When I asked Ford if Ezra was a gentleman, Ford answered that of course he wasn't because he was an American. There was a time when I would've countered that with a stiff punch in the nose, with or without boxing gloves. But I passed and we continued to ask each other if so-and-so would have been considered a gentleman and why. I have a vague recollection of this afternoon, however, in my mind's eye it's a little out of focus, which may have been caused at the time by a whiskey or two. As noted Ford was a tough pill to swallow and often required a chaser. I think I remember him telling me that he was a gentleman and that I was not, but I can't believe I let that one go without a physical reaction—especially if I had a drink or two. He did tell me however that I was a promising young writer, probably to assuage the anger he saw rising in me. I do remember Ford announcing that Sir Henry Hotspur Humblethwaite and his creator Anthony Trollope were not gentleman. Somebody I knew had a photo of the Victorian era novelist and I remember he had a beard to rival Karl Marx or one or both of the Smith brothers or Wilkie Collins for that matter. I remember telling him that I thought Trollope was true to himself and his writing, and he was quite creative in his search for writing ideas. He had written some novels while working as a postal inspector, and from time to time he would pick through the 'lost letter' file for subject matter. Brilliant. He was also damned disciplined. He set very strict goals about how much he would write each day, stuck to them, and became extremely prolific. The game went on, Ford thought Fielding might be a gentleman and Marlowe wasn't and John Donne, a parson, won by default. Fielding who had been a magistrate and founded London's first police force, became engaged in a dalliance with a young lady which put him in trouble with the very persons he had helped to organize. Karma. I remember writing a letter to a professor somewhere in the states, where I used Fielding as an example of an intelligent writer—a rare breed indeed. I grouped him with Anatole France, Hardy, Knut Hamsun and Conrad—even with his blind spots. Anyway, that dichotomy involving Fielding could explain Ford's uncertainty when judging him. I can remember, however, arguing that the scales might've been tipped in favor of his not being a gentleman when he married his wife's pregnant maid soon after his wife had passed away. His exceptional work as a magistrate probably saved his gentlemanly bacon. Christopher Marlowe died mysteriously at the young age of 29. He had been arrested on some heresy charge relating to a manuscript of his and 10 days later he was stabbed to death thereby, according to Ford, automatically removing him from gentlemanly contention. His murder was never solved. Ezra, and this was one of those times I couldn't tell whether he was serious or not, said that there was just a chance that Marlowe had faked his death and continued writing plays that he gave to Shakespeare in as much as his own reputation would have pretty much ruined his chances of being published or performed. Ford finally left the Lilas way past the time it would have been prudent for him to do so. Emile, another waiter/friend like Jean, and I returned to perusing the local racing forms.

Soon after Ford had left, the intriguing caped man and the enchanting tall woman once again walked by the window going in the other direction. And I am sitting there thinking its Belloc because of the pronouncements of the lightweight who has just blessed me with his departure. So I make the mistake of showing off my newfound knowledge by telling another patron that Hilaire Belloc has just walk by the window. The fellow tells me not to be an ass, that it wasn't Belloc at all, and that the fellow would be ripped if he had heard me identify him as such. He told me that it had been Aleister Crowley—a real nutcase. I asked him who the tall femme fatale was and he tells me it's probably one of Crowley's witches and states with a good degree of certainty that he is supposed to be the wickedest man alive, which made me think he probably wouldn't pass Ford's true gentleman test. I really didn't know Crowley but I saw him several times after that. He was hard to miss. He was a presence. I just remember a blue Italian infantry Cape and a stare that was just short of out-of-control. I had heard, however, a lot of stories about him from both Sylvia and Miss Stein and others. The tales were legion and one was stranger than the next.

He was English and described as an occultist and a magician. His motto was something along the lines of 'ordinary morality is only for ordinary people' which spoke to his extraordinary libertine ways. He was always getting thrown out of places, including Italy in 1923. Some of us referred to Wedderkop as Mr. Dear Awfully Nice, if that were true then Crowley was Mr.

Counterculture. He was a Satanist which, even on the liberal left bank of the Seine, put more than a few people off. My litmus test in matters like these was always Hadley, and she did not even like hearing about this man. Miss Stein, however, was fascinated by him and I have to admit to that, myself. But he was a strange one whose reasoning was not so reasonable. One of his paintings, that he called *May Morn,* used to give me nightmares. I can still see the red headed corpse hanging from a tree. He claimed to be the worst man in the world and no one disputed him. Perhaps his most outrageous moment was when he claimed to be invisible. Too bad Ford wasn't, in fact if I got going this could be a long list. In my notes I ended this sketch with xxx at the bottom of the page which is the way reporters used to end their submissions. Over the years xxx changed to—30—which I guess is someone's translation of the Roman numeral."

ECOLE LES LILAS

Ernest awoke on a clear Cuban morning. The temperature was in the mid-70s and the humidity in the mid-50s, but their forecast was to increase whereas he would lessen. He dressed himself slowly in tan cotton shorts and a white guayabera and sat down, exhausted. Looking out the window over some of the 15 acres of his Cuban "lookout farm", he pictured himself in khakis and a checkered flannel shirt in his extravagant second-floor bedroom and thought about how much Idaho could look like Michigan. Lately if he'd close his eyes, it would take him a beat or two to remember where he was. It was unnerving and not unusual for him to mentally visit assorted homes frequently. He had grown up in a seven bedroom Oak Park home that had a doctor's office for his father and a music studio for his mother. They had also owned a summer cottage on Walloon Lake in Michigan where his father had taught him, as early as four years old, the outdoors. They would go camping in the woods and hunt and fish. He was an outdoorsman from early on and continued to be so for the rest of his life. From 1913 to 1917 he went to Oak Park and River Forest High School where he tried his hand at running, water polo, a little football and boxing, which he seemed to favor. He did well in English and took journalism, wrote articles and edited the school newspaper and yearbook as a junior. Like Sinclair Lewis, who he would run into as an expat in Paris, he was a journalist first. After high school he went to work for the Kansas City Star as a reporter and was directed to use short, direct sentences, short paragraphs, robust English and to be positive rather than negative. This was good advice which he followed. He did not go to college but rather saw World War

I as his secondary education, which had everything to do with him telling Scott Fitzgerald that every good writer needed a war in his life. He was with the Kansas paper for about six months before signing on as an ambulance driver in Italy early in 1918. He had tried numerous times to enter the war, but had been rejected because of his eyesight. In May he went from New York to Paris, which at the time was being shelled by the Germans, and a month later he was at the Italian front where his legs were severely wounded and he earned a medal for bravery. He was a hero at age 18. He spent six months in the Milan hospital where he met a Red Cross nurse seven years his senior named Agnes von Kurowsky. He was smitten and had indications that she was as well. In January 1919 he was released and returned to the states. They had decided that marriage was in their future when he left Milan, but the young hero was not immune from heartbreak, as he received his first Dear John letter on March 7, 1919 when Agnes told him she was engaged to an Italian officer. He may have sworn to himself that he would never allow that to ever happen again which may have had something to do when he left Hadley for Paula, Paula for Martha and Martha for Mary. He married Hadley in September 1921 when he was 22. So about the time he would have graduated from college, he had been educated by vocation, war and love. For him it had been a new kind of school. He sat at his desk in Cuba and began writing what would become chapter 10 in *A Moveable Feast*.

"In one of the notebooks, my own handwriting tells me that one afternoon I was in the Lilas, minding my own writing. I was really getting after it. I was in Michigan and I could smell the pine trees, the lake—and even if I had to sharpen my pencil or start on a new lined notebook—I could get right back to the woods and my walk. I could feel my backpack, feel the weight and shape of it and smell the pine needles I put on my shoulder under the leather pack straps. As I walked, the pine would be worked between my shoulders and the straps and give off a crisp, pleasant, green scent. I could also feel the needles under my shoes as they walked to the lake.

"I had my luck with me. My pants' pocket luck. A buckeye and a rabbit's foot, but luck abandoned me suddenly as I was interrupted. And it wasn't the first time. I wasn't very kind about the interruption and I was hoping like hell that he wasn't planning on making this a permanent invasion by bringing his crowd to the Lilas on a regular basis. I closed the notebook and put down the pencil when he said hello and asked me if I was trying to write in a café. What the hell did it look like I was doing, milking the morning goat? I was thinking that Hadley would tell me to stay calm and kind and if she'd been there I might've held, but she wasn't and I didn't. I let him have it, called him a bad name and asked him what he was doing here and why he wasn't crawling in his usual sewers. He shot back, answered my insult with one of his own and then I told him to get his dirty camping mouth out. Hadley would've shivered and asked if we could leave but as I've said she wasn't there so I didn't. I hated critics which is how I saw him. People who were paid to have an attitude toward things, professional critics, usually make me sick. They're nothing more than the camp-following eunuchs of literature, all well-meaning and high-minded but in the end they are all just camp followers, sexual servants. He was like somebody standing behind you when you're fishing or looking over your shoulder when you're writing a letter to your best girl. But I didn't stop there. I had lost all of my temper. I told him to go back to the drag queen club I knew he frequented. I told him he belonged there. Then he said something like 'oh dear don't be so tiresome'. If I could write it in a lisp I would.

"I had been writing straight and simple and good. He had intruded, interfered. It even overcame my horse chestnut and rabbit's foot. Superstitions. Funny, but when I'm asked if I'm superstitious I usually say no—but I am and when I think about it, why is a rabbit's foot lucky? Why is a buckeye lucky? Ezra, who had a few superstitions of his own, told me that he carried a raccoon penis bone for good luck. I told him it wasn't lucky for the animal.

When I was growing up in Michigan, one time at the lake an old man told me to spit on the bait for luck. I tried it a few times but it didn't seem to work. Four leaf clover's had a good reputation but I didn't have the patience to mine them. Sylvia told me that a strange woman entering your home on New

Year's Day is good luck. I tried to encourage this in my own little apartment, but Hadley had her opinion and the experiment died on our doorstep. I got used to carrying a buckeye in Michigan. A lot of people from Ohio vacationed in Michigan and once a boy I met, who carried one for luck, gave it to me. It resembled a chestnut with a light circle in the center. He told me that Indians thought it looked like a male deer's eye—a buck's eye. Evidently they thought that buckeyes attracted deer. The rabbit's foot, on the other hand, was good luck for having a family among other things.

My brother Leicester had explained the prodigious reproduction reputation of the rabbit. I think he had written a term paper on it or something. If I'm remembering correctly rabbits become sexually mature in six months, it takes about a month from conception to birth, and rabbits can get pregnant the day after delivering a litter plus there can be 12 to a litter and they live to 10 years. I also remember that on one of my trips to Africa one of the natives on our Safari told me that the rabbit's foot was an important talisman to him. The fact that the rabbits live in burrows deep underground meant that they were in direct communication with the gods and spirits of the underworld.

But I think the best example of a charm or superstition that worked was the Indian rain dance. It was 100% effective. It worked every time and the reason it worked so well was that the Indians kept dancing until it rained.

"To protect my café, my writing place, my home away from home was very important to me then. The Lilas afforded a pleasant place to write, the waiters were top drawer and the people I came to know there would not bother me when I was writing. It was my home café—close, warm, cordial. And now there was an intruder. It was either go somewhere else or make a stand. I stood and I told this fellow, we'll call him Hal, as far as I know Hadley is the only other person who knows for sure who it was, to go back to the *Petite Chaumiere* where he belonged. He was a member of the Parisian gay subculture and I have already admitted to an unfortunate bias against homosexuality I had in Paris at the time. In fact given that, perhaps I should not include this chapter; but, on the other hand, that's the way I was then, even though I have changed my view. Back then there were several same-sex nightspots that everyone knew about. The Monocle was a prominent lesbian nightclub, though people like Miss Stein, Alice, Sylvia and Adrienne would not have gone there. Some 'fairy nice boys' as they were called, went to straight clubs like the Angel Bar, Liberty Bar or the *Champs Élysées Bar* where their acceptance was marginal. There was also, of course, a group of exclusively gay bars. The one I remember was the *Cousine* tucked in behind the *Moulin Rouge*. But the fellow who had just interrupted me spent most of his time at *La Petite Chaumiere* at 2 rue Berthe. It was a small cottage building which had windows covered in red, Cubist paintings on the walls, a piano and a lot of men in drag.

"I remember when he showed up and bollixed my writing regimen. There I was in the place, good place, warm, well lit, with good drinks and good waiters. And then something bad comes in. It can take many shapes, from an odor to a flood. Well that's what he was. Somewhere between an odor and a flood. This was my home field and I told him he could go elsewhere. I wanted to punch his nose but he actually sat down and had a drink. It was sort of like throwing down the gauntlet. I tried to write with him there. It had been going so well, straight and simple, that the sentences were still coming despite him. He kept trying to start a conversation and finally I finished the thought I had and wrote the first sentence on the next and put down the pencil. He kept carping. But I had proved to myself I could write even if the plague sat nearby. I had lived through Ezra murdering the bassoon when he was using it to help him write opera. The Pounds lived at 70 Notre-Dame-des-Champs and we lived at 113, a distance unfortunately easily traveled by the notes of the bassoon, not quite enough real estate to blunt the discord especially when the ambient noise of the street had died. So I knew a few things about noise up close and personal. Ezra also had a carpenter's workshop and I had lived with that cacophony. Hal did not rise to the level of a cacophony but somehow he managed to get deeper under the skin. I went on writing. I felt the buckeye and rabbit's foot kick in. He kept whining. Aside from Ezra's musical malpractice and his carpenter shop, Hadley and I lived above a lumber mill and somehow Hal's constant chatter exceeded even the decibel output of the mill motor and that large circular blade going to war with timbers. Then finally he gave me an opening too sweet to pass up. He told me he'd gone to Greece. It was time for a homophone in more ways than one. I should have resisted but I didn't. Once again Hadley's disappointment would've been swift and justified. 'Did you use it or go there?' He told me not to be vulgar. I had been and I would be. He wanted to tell me more. He wanted to talk to me until the seasons changed. I finally just smiled a faint smile and packed up my pencil and paper to go home. In a last gasp he told me he was looking for help as a writer. I told him I probably could help him best by shooting him. He treated that like a glancing blow and kept on coming with more chatter but then he gave me another opening. 'I'd do anything for you,' he said. Music to my besieged ears. I took him at his word and asked him to stay away from the Lilas. It wasn't his kind of establishment anyway and he promised he'd stay away. At last we had a contract. I was feeling better. In my weakness, however, I dropped my guard. I became neighborly and asked him what he was writing. Of all the questions, in all the gin joints, why did I have to ask that one? He whined some more about how difficult it was to write. I tried a little common sense, 'you shouldn't write if you can't write'. I think I actually told him to hang himself, or get a job but for God's sake to stop whining. I told him he never could write, which was the truth. Then I added that he should shut up. Then he got cranked up and the rules of engagement changed. He got vulgar, mephitic and murderous. He told me I was cruel, heartless and conceited and that he had always defended me but no more. If he defended like he danced, I was not losing much.

"Then we had a breakthrough, a detente. I suggested he try being a critic. He took it like a trout takes a fly. He asked if I thought he would be good at it. I told him there would be people who would help him and as a critic he could help his friends. I called them his own people. They were writers. He said they already had critics. I told him there was more to being a critic than just books. There were paintings, plays, dances, films and more. I could tell by the look on his face that he was already conceiving of himself as a critic. So I offered this critic without papers a drink. He took the drink and then in a move I should have foreseen, he began criticizing my writing style. I remembered the gold ring I had with the word equanimity engraved inside. I was grasping for peace under pressure but it was elusive. 'Your writing is too clipped, too lean but don't go too far the other way either,' he chided. When he was through reproaching, disparaging, castigating, reprimanding, fulminating—pick one—I cited our recent contract and reminded him not to invade the Lilas when I was writing. He agreed. He said he'd have his own café now. In his mind he was already a successful critic holding court somewhere. It didn't take long, he was on his way—unfortunately it never worked out for him, outside of his mind. For good measure as he walked out I reminded him that it was many times more difficult to create than to criticize.

"The next sketch in the notebook following my dust-up with Hal, was a scene with me in the morning in our apartment with Bumby and the cat and the baby bottles—much better, more comfortable in my own environs. That particular day I was writing clean and true and I didn't need the rabbit's foot on the buckeye—but I carried them anyway for insurance. I was at the Lilas and I had my schoolboy notebook and pencil and was secure in the knowledge that the lesson I had learned the day before proved to me that writing in the Lilas was good, very accessible and pleasant. I also learned that I needed to protect it from incursions by the likes of Hal and that with no one bothering me, I could transport myself to Michigan or Switzerland or anywhere else. And I thought there would always be new things to learn and that I had found a new school and I would remember it as *L' Ecole Les Lilas.*

PASCIN

Before going to bed he stared at the gazelles staring back from the fieldstone fireplace. There were antelope here in Idaho in the river valley a few hours away but now that felt almost as far away as Africa. He stepped outside and could hear the Big Wood River. He had been coming here for 30 years, first with Martha then Mary; maybe, he thought, it would end here. He couldn't sleep. He rolled over. He still couldn't sleep. Parts of him ached, but it was the worry, the almost constant worry that kept him from sleeping. He was slipping, sometimes down, sometimes sideways. The direction wasn't always clear but the slipping, the drift, the fall was. He hadn't failed at much in his life—Agnes back in 1918 Spain—and then there was the matter of three marriages that went south—but after those not so much. But his marriage was failing now, and he was failing now, seriously failing, failing for keeps. At some moments, when he was confused, it was almost a freefall. He would capsize and slip back and he cursed himself when he did.

He sensed the writing on the wall but it wasn't his writing. The doctors, the men in white coats, were failing him like the first doctor in his life had failed him, his father. His father had embarrassed him by killing himself. He considered it an act of cowardice. It was like Sartre's play, there was no exit. He was glad to have the Paris book to write. The notes he took so long ago still gave him comfort. There was solace and assuagement in the remembering, even though it was more palliative than not.

"Hi Papa", Mary said, in her dressing gown, with her hands behind her back. She was trying to keep it light.

"Hi kitten", he answered slowly. "I'm going to work here this morning. I think I can get 400 words, in fact I'm sure I can." They were attempting to make this a pleasant day, an island in a stream of troubled ones.

"Good", she said, and from behind her back she produced a black bowler hat. "Look what I found." She put it on. It was too big. She looked like a burlesque act in her dressing gown and bowler hat. She had a pixie-like grin and looked, if she had a cane, like she could soft shoe across the enormous bedroom in the house overlooking the river.

"That's an old hat," he said remembering.

"It sure looks it," she winked, relieved to see him engaged. More often than not, he wasn't. "It's an old hat and it smells a lot like your notebooks."

"In fact it's very old. You're right it was in one of the trunks. It was a gift. A gift from a friend who always wore one. He put it on my head one night at the Dome in Montparnasse. In those days you could get a sausage and potatoes for a dollar. We all went there." His voice trailed off.

"Who gave it to you?" She asked holding the hat now in her hands.

"Pascin."

"This is Pascin's hat?"

"Was."

"Tell me the story?" she asked genuinely interested.

"The painters we knew all had pretty models that they painted nude or almost nude and we were quite sure, though we didn't speak of it much, that there was more than just painting going on. Most of them slept with them, saying it added to the painting. I had wondered on occasion if I had a nude young girl sitting next to me while I wrote, if it would make the book easier to write. But that idea would have been derailed before it left the station. At any rate it was one of those good mornings in Paris when I was working well. I worked hard and long until late in the afternoon and finally put on a jacket I had brought from Canada and walked past the rail car and the lumber stacked against our building. Once I had my picture taken there and the piled wood made an amusing texture for the background. I cut through the bread-scented bakery. Had I been blindfolded I would have known easily when the *pâtisserie* was near. They had been baking in that building for a very long time and every splinter of wood in it had the bakeshop bouquet. The tired sun hurried to the horizon and twilight was lit. Shadow herded in the nightfall and I walked to a café that Ezra had recommended. He called it Lavigne's—I can't remember its real name. It was positive and welcoming and kind to the pocket. The special was a cassoulet with duck confit, duck sausage and duck bacon with beans tomatoes and onions. It was one of the few meals that on its own filled me completely. Ezra's wife Dorothy had told me about the meal. She thought I would like it and she couldn't have been more right. Ezra's wife was born Dorothy Shakespear—without the final e—but with a serious face and a twinkle. We took her suggestions about books and plays and such very seriously, as if she were the bard, and Sylvia showed her deference to make kind fun. And as I have said her culinary endorsements were spot on. The manager of the café whose name was Lavigne could have given Hal the intruder a lesson in café manners. He told me he had seen me working at the Lilas but did not speak to me as he did not want to be an annoyance, *a contrariete.* What very good sense. To be honest, people went to cafés to eat, drink and talk to others, and then some would go just to be seen by others, and for some time I had to examine my motives.

"I had worked hard all day and thought that I had earned an evening out. In fact I even thought of going out to the races but that seemed a bit extravagant so I thought I would save the money from the race track and go to a nice dinner. It was a game. Some days I skipped lunch so I could have a whiskey. Other days I would skip this so I could do that. It was trading. Or if Miss Stein's formula were to be followed, you don't buy the clothes you need, but you save the money and buy a painting. But the café that Ezra and Dorothy had suggested was nice and had an interesting red wine. It was a Malbec and a particular favorite of mine. Malbec grapes grown in Cohorn made a first-rate wine that you could cut with water and still enjoy. In those days wines that were strong enough to stand up to a mix of water were a boon to everyone's budget. The taste of this red was athletic, the consequence robust.

"But Papa, I thought you were going to tell me a story about this old hat."

"This is what's called the run-up. I'm merely preparing you for the story. Trying to build a little suspense. We're out here in the middle of Idaho with nothing but nature around, we have no appointments that I know of so stay with me and I will make the story worthwhile."

"We have a contract."

"Anyway it was about this time in either the Dome, the Select or the Rotonde that I ran into Harold Stearns, and when I did, I felt a small pinch of guilt. He was a Harvard man, journalist, essayist, editor and critic. He helped me get published. He was the one who actually talked Liveright into putting out *In Our Time*. I never thanked him quite enough. As it turned out I don't think I ever thanked anyone quite enough. Somebody—it might've been Scott, or Dos—described Stearns as a picturesque ruin, but he had helped me and I owed him. Stearns drank like a Viking and was a fixture at the Select. He worshipped champagne and when he'd had enough champagne, he'd drink more champagne. I'd seen him pass out more than twice, but he knew horses and could pick a winner once in a while.

"Hang on we're getting to the good part. I walked into the Dome which had more than its share of artists and their models. The models were not unattractive. In the late afternoon, the good light would retreat from the studios and the artists and their models would retire to the Dome. At that time I knew Jules Pascin. He was known as the Prince of Montparnasse. His surname was really Pincas, but his family was upset and embarrassed at the nudes he was sketching and did not want to be associated with his art, so for their sake he changed his name to Pascin which is an anagram of Pincas. I liked him—the Prince—for many reasons. He had talent and was immune from the critics. He was an experimenter, with art, with people, with a lot of things. He always wore a bowler and it suited him. It was his trademark. He was very generous and spent as much as he made. He threw great parties and picnics and always had a surprise. He waved me into the Dome. He did not have to do it twice. He was flanked by two very good-looking bookends. A dusty and drunk tome bordered by two temptresses. He offered me a drink which was his custom. I accepted, which was mine. He said that it was a good night and he had a lot of money. The smart wager would be that he left the Dome with empty pockets. He looked to his left and asked if I wanted to take the dark haired seductress to bed. The two models were sisters and the dark-haired one's name was Bronia Perlmutter. My notes were very specific about Bronia. She had short, dark hair parted in the middle, wide set melancholy eyes and cherub lips like Clara Bow. She wore black strapped shoes, a pleated skirt and a checked jacket with a small white scarf. She carried a small music box with three ballerinas on top that swirled when the music played. I didn't say yes, but I didn't say no. So we sat there in an awkward silence. Awkward for everyone but Pascin. I never saw him awkward, the word wasn't in his vocabulary and he couldn't have spelled it, I don't think, if you gave him the letters and a head start. The sisters sat there. They were still posing, maybe they never stopped. First they would show off this, then that. It was altogether pleasurable. He told the dark one she looked like a toy doll from Java—she told him he was too old to play with toys, but the argument was not mean.

"She asked me if I liked her and I told her I did. I was not thinking of anyone but myself. There were too many times that I only thought of myself and this was one of those times. She told me I looked too big for her and I said something that I would like to blame on the drink, but that would not be true. I told her that everyone is the same size in bed and I said it with what felt like a grin. Then the sisters told their artist that they wanted to eat and asked if I were going with them. I told them I was going home to eat with my family. It was somewhat difficult to think of my apartment in this situation. But I kept thinking of it as the three of them carried each other toward the door. The last thing Pascin did before walking out was to turn and place his hat on my head. It didn't fit real well but it felt like a trophy.

"Years later, when he hanged himself, I was asked to say a few words at his memorial service, and after I had told everyone what a lovely painter he was, I told them that I liked to remember him as he was that night at the Dome in his black bowler hat. I also told them that they say the seeds of what we will do are in all of us, and I remembered as I did so, that my father and Hadley's father had both taken their own lives and that my mother had given me as a birthday gift the gun my father used to end his life."

Mary looked at him and felt sad.

EZRA POUND & T. S. ELIOT

This morning he actually didn't hurt so much though he felt mildly confused. He found if he concentrated on one thing he would do okay. Today that one thing would be Ezra.

Among the reported 7000 books shelved in the rooms of the Finca, were no fewer than 50 books and poems by TS Eliot. Among his favorites, The *Wasteland,* which he read many Aprils, *Prufrock,* the reference-laden *Ash Wednesday, The Hollow Men* with its memorable "not with a bang but a whimper" ending and finally *Old Possum* which was Ezra's nickname for Eliot. He also liked Eliot's cat book because later in life he had become an ailurophile. Ernest admired all of Eliot's work and he loved Eliot but he didn't love him as much as Ezra loved the Old Possum.

He was up earlier than usual, bitching at the owl that had kept him awake, and by the time he dressed, a ritual not near as automatic or easy as it once was, coffee and bread were on the long table in the middle of the morning sunlit dining room. A large green cockroach scurried by and he tried to get it with his foot but didn't even come close. "Day was I could catch those on the first try even when they flew and I was half full of rum", he remembered. One of his favorite cats, named for Christopher Columbus, rubbed against his leg as he sat down heavily in the thick wooden chair across from Miro's "Finca". A paper-clipped draft of the current chapter was on the table beneath a copy of the October, 1922 edition of *The Criterion*, an English literary journal that had published Eliot's "Wasteland". It had been in one of the trunks. He picked up the draft and began to read.

"One of the Paris notebooks had almost five pages full of a drama that played out in our neighborhood having to do with Ezra and his desire to free Eliot from his job which would then enable him to spend full-time writing. I had asked Ezra once about the nickname he had for Eliot and all he said was 'phalangeriformes'. It was the scientific name for possum, but it hurt my lips to pronounce so I didn't pursue that line of questioning. Pound's nickname was Brer Rabbit, both names being taken from *Uncle Remus*—brainchild of Joel Chandler Harris—which had been around since the late 1800s.

"Ezra and Eliot actually wrote to each other in Uncle Remus dialects, so we know that at least once in a while they had too much time on their hands. Suffice it to say that they were the greatest of friends, although once Ezra challenged him to a duel—but then he and Eliot were always challenging someone to a duel.

"At that time in Paris, some of us were having trouble balancing our desire to write with our desire to eat. Me for instance. Hadley had about $3000 a year in inheritance coming in and I was working for the Toronto Star. But things were tight and when I quit the paper, things were tighter. I was looking to sell poems, stories, anything. Well along comes Ezra and says that Eliot, who he worshiped as a poet, needed to quit his job in order to be free to write. Yeah, I thought, didn't we all.

"Ezra had printed up a handout suggesting a five year pledge of $250 payable at $50 per year. Ezra wanted us all to pitch in to buy TS out of his banking job. Well, some of us had a smaller pitch than others, but I put some money aside thinking maybe this was a model that would, in turn, help us all. In retrospect I think I might have used some of those funds for whiskey or a horse that didn't come home. Well in the middle of this exercise, Eliot, who as it turned out really didn't want to quit his job after all, caught fire and had more money than all of us. There was intrigue surrounding these two and I found a manuscript I'd started in our apartment above the saw mill."

He wiped his glasses on the linen napkin and began reading to himself. Reading it to Mary would not bear fruit, Hadley was too much in this sketch. "Interesting, sitting here I've just convinced myself that this would make a chapter in the Paris book. He began to type.

"The man who had measured out his life with coffee spoons means a lot to Ezra," I said sitting in our apartment and removing my glasses.

"What does that mean Tati?" Hadley asked.

"We'll have to ask Ezra to be sure."

"I like Ezra. He's good and kind and so very helpful. And Dorothy too. Don't you think she's pretty, Tati?"

"I do."

"Ezra and Dorothy may have been the only friends Hadley and I had who lived more humbly than we did. It was a small studio on our street and it had a stove and good Northern light to work by. It was decorated with Japanese art and Dorothy's paintings which I liked because I liked her and I liked her because she was lovely and kind and sculpted. There was also a rough-hewn bust of Ezra by Henri Gaudier-Brzeska, a French sculptor and artist whose painting style was influenced by Dorothy's paintings. Hadley asked me if Ezra was the smartest man on our street. I changed the subject and she smiled. She said that Ezra had told her that literature was news that stayed news and she told me she thought that was quite good. I agreed, I wished I'd said it.

"You know Ezra likes Picabia's paintings," I said for no particular reason.

"You don't like them very well do you Tati?"

"No, he was an avant-garde everything. His paintings look like he's lying to himself."

"But they are colorful and rich and make you think."

"I don't like anything about them. They hurt. And Ezra also likes Wyndham's."

"And you don't?" She predicted.

"And I don't. His painting of Ezra shows him slouched in a chair asleep in a rumpled suit and tie. It doesn't do him justice, besides everyone is furthering a movement like Picabia and Dadaism or inventing a school like Lewis and Vorticism. It was short-lived. It should have been shorter lived. It tried to take Cubism a step further when it didn't need another step. I just don't understand."

"But I think Ezra does," she said, turning from the window.

"Ezra is loyal, he likes the works of his friends."

"Isn't that good?" She asked, "To be loyal to one's friends."

"Yes, if it's true, but to like the bad art of a friend is false."

"You like Dorothy's paintings?" She asked and concluded at the same time.

"I do."

"Because she's your friend and neighbor or because she is beautiful, or because her art is good?"

"For all three," I said, and walked into the bedroom for my jacket.

"I thought highly of Ezra. He was a good friend, neighbor, writer and one of the kindest persons I knew. Hadley and I had agreed one night at Michaud's that in the end it all came down to kindness and I called Ezra a saint. Hadley had never heard me call anyone a saint—not even the real ones. But saints evidently do not make good boxers because I tried hard to teach him that sport but to no avail. I was no fan of Wyndham Lewis. I thought he looked like a frog smoking a cigarette, and I thought he dressed to be a spectacle. Unfortunately I probably used a boxing session with Ezra, that Lewis watched, as an excuse to show off to everyone that I was a boxer and knew the nomenclature of the sport, and as an opportunity to tell everyone how despicable Lewis was.

"I remember on more than one occasion claiming Lewis had the eyes of an unsuccessful rapist or a cornered virgin or some such loathsome analogy. A lot of the stories in the 1926 notebooks could be called revenge pieces—but Lewis held a special place in my malevolent hierarchy.

"Miss Stein and I found a way to disagree forever but we did agree on Wyndham Lewis. She had a better name for him than anything I had contrived. Actually I think Alice might have come up with it but, regardless, the appellation was 'the measuring worm'. This insult described how he would devise to copy someone's painting by measuring it up and seeing exactly how it was done—but he could never quite pull it off.

"I've tried to help some of our group, Hem," Ezra said with way too much humility. Truth known he had helped us all, bar none, the lot of us. "I've tried to help some of us, but I've found someone who really needs help and I can't do it by myself. Now I need help." Needless to say I would give up races and whiskey for a week to answer Ezra's call.

"Who needs the help?" I asked.

"Tom Eliot," we need to bail him out of his position at the bank so that he can write. He's a writer, a great writer, not a bloody banker."

In 1917 TS Eliot had taken a job at Lloyd's bank. It was this position to which Ezra so strenuously objected. Ezra said Eliot needed to be freed from the brass cage of Lloyd's to give him the time to write. To accomplish this, Ezra founded his *Bel Esprit* or 'beautiful spirit' with another expat, Natalie Clifford Barney. She held salons at her address on rue Jacob and introduced many members of the lost generation to each other.

"Miss Barney was a lesbian like Gertrude or Alice but more attractive, on the order of Sylvia Beach or Adrienne Monnier. Ezra and Natalie were consumed with the idea of purchasing TS Eliot's freedom from the shackles of his banking profession. I accepted this premise when I thought that, after Tom Eliot was gifted with enough money enabling him to write, the rest of the expats in the same situation, in turn, would receive the same benefit. But soon it became clear that this program was tailored for Tom with no plans to extend it or broaden its scope. They attempted to raise funds for TS until he won the Dial prize for *The Wasteland* after which Tom Eliot's worth started to look like Lloyds'.

In 1920 *The Dial* was an American literary magazine. The magazine paid Eliot $2130 for the poem and also awarded him the magazine's annual prize of $2000. The poem or prize alone nearly equaled Eliot's 1922 Lloyd's salary of $2215. The need for *Bel Esprit*, at least for TS Eliot, had vanished. *Bel Esprit* followed shortly thereafter and Eliot left Lloyds in 1925.

"As I have said before, I love both Ezra and TS Eliot and I love their poetry but I did take exception to a notion they each expressed in verse. Ezra had written a poem called *And the Days Are Not Full Enough*. It's a short poem, only four lines and the last two are as follows, 'and life slips by like a field mouse / not shaking the grass'. Eliot wrote, *The Hollow Men* the last two lines of which read, 'this is the way the world ends / not with a bang but a whimper'. Well with all respect to my two good friends, to hell with life slipping by like a field mouse without shaking the grass and to hell with this is the way the world ends, not with a bang but a whimper. Bullshit. When it's my turn I'm going out with a bang—no whimpering, no slipping by like a field mouse careful not to shake the grass.

"When reading other expats' writing, I used to get the idea that it might be fun to try to write something in the style of another writer. Take James Joyce an example. I was thinking of writing one of these chapters in the Paris book in the stream of consciousness but it would be a false thing and probably not very entertaining. So I decided to leave that to Joyce—he is expert at interior monologue and free association, although Nora once told him he should write a book that somebody could read and that his stream of consciousness had flooded. I'll always love her for that.

"When TS Eliot's ship came in at *The Dial, Bel Esprit* folded. Ezra and Miss Barney smiled at each other, felt good about what they had done, had champagne and moved on; and, as I believe I mentioned, I took the money set aside for the cause and dropped most of it into that ravenous abyss known as the racetrack. The racetrack was hungry enough to eat a horse, and it ate mine … all of them.

ADIEU MISS STEIN

"Here I was in Cuba with more than half of the Paris book at least in first draft. The word around Paris amongst the expats was that the first draft of anything was *merde*. But I had enough written and the rest outlined and organized that I knew I could finish this book, even though my faculties were failing. If my condition wasn't enough to scare the hell out of me, the condition of Cuba was."

Castro had chased Batista into the Dominican largely on the promise of a "free Cuba" but here, ten months in, communists from Venezuela were taking government positions. Ernest had met an attractive young Cubano who had played a central role in the revolution. In fact at times he was as popular as Castro. His name was Camilo Cienfuegos and Ernest had met him in Havana at the Floridita, a bar and restaurant across from the museum of fine arts where they have been serving daiquiris since they invented them in 1930. In the relatively short time they were together, the two soldiers had a conversation about death. The Cuban hero, whose picture was everywhere with Fidel and Che, admitted that he had a premonition he would die young. Ernest had already outlived that forewarning, but confessed to similar thoughts when he was Camilo's age and younger. At their meeting, Ernest was 60 and Camilo 27, and the old man felt a hint of fatherhood getting to know the handsome young soldier with good wit who didn't fear death. Both men, strangely enough, were suspicious of communism. Ernest had met Fidel only once at a fishing tourney and suggested to Camilo, once it was clear they were *simpatico* on the issue, that he had not been without some doubts when meeting the *commandante*. Over rums Camilo asked a lot of questions about literature. He professed wanting to be a writer, but had been surprised at how much he had enjoyed being a soldier and even more so when Castro had put him in charge of the revolutionary army. Camilo wasn't exactly sure of the author's politics; but he didn't care, he had the good fortune to be seated next to a famous author. He told Ernest, "My head is full of ideas, one after another, but they serve no purpose in my head. I must put them down on paper." Ernest then gave him some tips on doing just that. They spoke in Spanish and Camilo noted, "It is not difficult to write in Spanish, the language is a gift from the gods. Literature is best used to express the joy and wisdom of mankind, it is an art form of all and for all, heeding only the voiceless, anonymous murmur of a given place and time."

The old man pursed his lips and raised his eyebrows and his glass, "By God that was well said … I think you just might have what it takes my young friend … just might have it." They touched glasses and Hemingway smiled remembering in a different land, a different language, a different time. Spurred on by the compliments and the Bacardi, Cienfuego explained that his family had come from Spain prior to the civil war. Ernest was only too pleased to recount some of his Spanish maneuvers. René had been waiting for a good time to remind Ernest that they should probably call it an evening. Camilo was explaining in words modified by rum that his favorite things to do were baseball, dancing and women.

"The first two are not on my list, but the third, well, that has a list all its own." Camilo laughed a million peso smile and hugged the old man and the old man hugged back. René signaled and Ernest left with a chorus of *hasta luegos*.

After their barroom meeting, Ernest followed reports of Camilo and was genuinely effected when, on a flight from Camaguey to Havana on the night of October 28, 1959, his Cessna 310 went into the sea. Even today the Cuban school children throw flowers into the Atlantic, Caribbean, Gulf of Mexico and the Windward Passage to honor him. So it was with thoughts of the spirited young Cuban no longer alive that Ernest carried himself back to Paris when he was that age.

"Even though the Hemingways and the Steins had parted ways and my feelings toward her were not what they once were, as I sit here today reading more transcriptions and some of those that were even typed out in the '20s, I find that I still have more material on Gertrude Stein than most everybody else. My relationship with her was always a qualified friendship. So maybe I'll try one more chapter with a final kiss goodbye to Miss Stein.

"Well Miss Stein had instructed me on sex and she had her model T ignition repaired and discovered the lost generation under the hood, and now I was going to deal with how it all concluded. At first it had been cordial enough. First with me and then Hadley and I and then even walks with Hadley and I and Bumby. Hell. Alice and Gertrude were his godparents. What was I thinking? I know exactly what I was thinking. Miss Stein was the center of the expat world. Doling out invitations and connections like a one lady PR firm. She was important and had means and the two of them would be at the center of things for a long time to come and would probably be laid to rest in *Pere Lachaise* with the other bright lights of the Paris nights.

"She had helped me and I had helped her. In truth, her advice, guidance, loans and connections more than counterbalanced my typing and proofreading of her manuscript and even helping get her book serialized with Ford. And she was gracious when things were going well. I could stop by, at almost any time but usually in the afternoon, and their maid Helene would look after me.

Sometimes when invited—and this happens to everyone—you would rather not go, for many reasons or for no reason at all. Turning down an invitation is always thin ice, ringed with pitfalls it is a high risk venture. I was not good at it and Hadley refused to tell an untruth to avoid it, so we went to a lot of events that I would rather have skipped. Hadley would say something like if you want the truth, I'll tell you the truth and the truth is I don't want to tell you the truth. That's how truthful she was. It got more perplexing than it had to I think. But Picasso taught me.

"His advice to me was that he always said yes and that I

should always say yes, always accept with no exceptions, especially the rich, they could buy his paintings or help me with a book. He explained that when you say yes the potential hosts are so pleased, you can see it on the mask they are wearing. They light up. You can always tell them later that something arose, some near crisis or crisis or misfortune or unforeseen mishap is upon you and you are as contrite as you can be and you apologize with feeling and everything is good again. Basically his formula was always say yes even if you know you're going to say no later. Keep your options open. I told him that Hadley would probably not approve of his program, and knowing as I did so, that he could probably now tell that I was not the one in charge at my little apartment. His advice to that, was don't tell her, and that my writing or Bumby or something else would wash away the dust stirred up by such a manipulation. I liked Picasso a lot and I listened to what he said. After all he was almost 20 years my senior, old enough to be my father really, and he should know more—and he did.

"Helene opened the door as if in anticipation of me, like she had been glancing through the cream colored curtains and saw me approaching. I had been there countless times before but for some reason I was hesitant this time. I was offered a seat and told that Miss Stein would be downstairs soon. It was early in the day but Helene poured me a brandy—perhaps it was reflexive on her part—Hemingway is here, get the brandy. I can remember this scene like it was a lot more recent than 30 years ago. Helene just poured me a solid *eau-de-vie* which I was flirting with, and just as I put it to my lips all hell broke loose upstairs. Miss Stein was beseeching, screeching, supplicating and what she said almost made me spill my brandy—in fact I think I did spill my brandy. It also made me think that next to what I'd just heard, *Up in Michigan* seemed like a grade school dance.

"As best I can remember and what the notes reflect is as follows: 'Don't Pussy. Please Pussy don't. Don't, please don't. I'll do whatever you want. Anything but please don't do it. Please Pussy I beg you, no.' I swallowed the brandy to keep from choking on it, put the empty glass down on the glass top mahogany side table with a small brass rail running around it like a fence. I headed for the door. Not only could I hear Miss Stein's shrill screams ringing in my ears, I could also hear Helene calling me back. 'Don't go, it'll be all right, really—she'll be down soon.' The Paris notes aren't clear as to what I said next nor do I remember exactly but it was something like, I really should go, thinking all the while that I had to get the hell out of there. I think I remember wondering what Picasso would do in this predicament, and then in my mind's ear I could almost hear him whispering, 'What the hell is taking you so long to get out of there?' So I did. As I opened the door I could hear the upstairs conversation crashing down to the first floor, deteriorating in decorum but not volume. It was an exchange right out of the sewer or the slop jar. I did tell the maid that I had to go, that I had a sick friend. This was by courtesy of the Spanish Cubist. It was Picasso's ready-made excuse. I told Helene to please tell Gertrude and Alice to have a good trip and travel well and that I would write to them, and please tell them I'm sorry I couldn't wait but I have to be elsewhere. Picasso would've been proud.

"At the bottom of the page in the notebooks where this sketch is written, is a note about Picasso being superstitious. I had forgotten all about this but when he had his fingernails cut or his hair trimmed he would save the clippings in a bag to be disposed of later. When I asked him about it once, he gave me an odd look and said that he didn't want anyone doing strange things with it. I really didn't know what he was talking about, but I didn't push it because the look he gave me told me not to. But what seems like a lifetime later, on a trip to Africa, I heard of natives putting curses on people by obtaining clips of their hair or fingernails. Perhaps Pablo should've carried a buckeye and a rabbit's foot, although now that I think of it his luck held pretty well."

ERNEST WALSH

Mary drove him the nine miles to Cojimar where Gregorio was waiting with the *Pilar.* She kissed him on the cheek and told him René would pick him up at five. He nodded. Gregorio was already smoking a cigar and had some fresh orange juice waiting. He asked if Papa wanted to fish, but sadly he declined. Lately he hadn't had the energy, and he was finding he could live off the memories. He was probably the premier bill fishermen in the world at this time, which was obviously no small feat, and it saddened him that his strength—something he had almost worshiped—was fading. He no longer had the stamina to strap himself into the fighting chair, hook the giant marlin and summon the force and intensity to war with the fish. "Not today amigo," he answered his friend and captain. He sipped at the juice and surveyed the Gulf. God it was beautiful, sun mining diamonds on the water, salt air in your lungs, wind in and out of your face with just a hint of Gregorio's Romeo and Juliet fresh from the blending room at the 160-year-old Partagas factory. Gregorio's eyes were the same color as the sea and his smile seemed to never end. "The *pescadores* are happy that you are back and look for you to visit La Terraza again."

Cojimar produces the best fishermen in Cuba and Ernest was legitimately in that group and was respected by the strong, dark-haired, weathered men of the sea who grew up no more than 10 miles from the Finca.

"Some have told me to tell you hello," Gregorio continued, "Anselmo, but he said he's already seen you, Bello Cachimba, El Sordo and El Soltero."

The names sounded like Spanish poetry to Ernest's dimmed

hearing. One of the great fishermen was named Tato which was very similar to the nickname Hadley had for him. Since he'd been reading the notebooks in his own hand and the typed versions Nita had finished, he had been thinking a lot about his first wife and how much he really had cared for her, though he'd been an unfaithful louse.

As he sat there in the bright sun of the Gulfstream with his old friend, he knew there was part of him—he wasn't sure where, he wasn't sure how big—but there was part of him that still loved Hadley. I can't un-love what I once loved, he said to himself and took off his glasses and wiped them.The next time he wrote about Hadley for the Paris book he would use the Corona typewriter that she had given him for his 22nd birthday. It was here at the Finca and sometimes so was she.

He sat there looking at the sunbaked, aged but sinewy body of his mate, and thought that just maybe the old Cuban knew more about him than anyone—not the sophisticated, art circles, Pulitzer, Nobel part, but the old man and the sea part. Hell, Gregorio was as much the old man and the sea as anyone.

He's seen me make a fool of myself, mostly over women, sometimes over drink, and he's seen the mighty tests with a huge billfish, and the boys, Bumby, Mouse and Gigi, and the wives and the other highs and lows but always the Gulfstream, the dark edge of the Gulfstream, always the cool breeze off the water and the strength of the *Pilar* beneath. He thought again of the fishermen.

"How many could we round up to meet us at La Terraza. I could buy them rums".

"That could be dangerous," Gregorio laughed, "We would have them coming in from Havana. More dangerous than going deep for the big fish or having Adrienne or Ava and the *señora* aboard together or even hunting U-boats," he made a swimming motion with his hand. Ernest belly laughed at his companion's definition of dangerous, but he had to admit it was pretty close to the mark. They were silent for a while listening to the engine, the water slapping the hull, the wind, the cry of a gull and also just the silence of the sea.

"Do you believe in God?" Gregorio asked him.

He was only two years older than Ernest and their birthdays were only 10 days apart in July. Both were considering their mortality, acknowledging the end, contemplating dealing with death. Clarence Hemingway had taught his son, up in Michigan, that humans were the only species that knew they were going to die—yet it didn't shroud people's lives in shadow—at least most people. But there was a question hanging in the air and he didn't want to offend his friend by not answering or by insulting what he guessed was a Catholic background. In truth he was not religious but he fashioned an answer for the situation.

"I believe in something, maybe it's myself, maybe it's my friends, maybe it's all people, maybe it's a thing called God, I don't know."

"I see," said Gregorio, not seeing it all. Ernest could remember thinking holy thoughts when he was staring death in the face, when he thought he might die. In Italy on the front with the mortar, and back to back plane crashes in Africa, in the brush fire out West. So religion for him, he thought, was situational and probably one of convenience and doubtless he would re-engage when he was one-on-one with extinction. But he hadn't been marked for death, at least not yet, he thought, like some he'd known.

Later that day after dinner, he and Mary were sitting in the living room with a drink. He had described the pleasant afternoon he had with Gregorio and was warming up for tomorrow morning's go at writing.

"You love that old Cuban don't you," Mary stated more than asked, sipping at a Cuban espresso.

"I do indeed, he's a good and decent man … I named Greg after him."

They were both quiet for a minute or so. Ernest had poured himself a sensible sized whiskey and was enjoying its smoky scent.

"Who was Santiago?" she asked. "I know Gregorio thinks it's him, I've heard him explain why. But what do you say? Who was Santiago for you?" She was not calling him Papa much anymore. Their deteriorating relationship made their exchanges less friendly, more remote. They both took another sip.

"It's a nice mystery to perpetuate ... it's a guessing game that some like." He took another sip, held it in his mouth, swallowed it and smiled briefly. "If St. Peter asks me who was Santiago and my admission hung in the balance and the truth was all I was allowed, then I would say that Carlos, who taught me much including how to fish from a skiff, was part of Santiago. Certainly Gregorio who has been with me for so long and was from the Canaries like the man in the book. Then there's Anselmo who was in fact the oldest fisherman in Cojimar when I wrote the story and who looked like he was straight from central casting. In fact I made sure Tracy met him before they started shooting. Marcos Puig had once gone 86 days without catching a fish and I used that. Mike Strater's catch is certainly in the book ... not that Mike is Santiago ... he's not ... but I remember thinking when we hauled in that hulking half fish that it would be part of the story." He paused to sip his drink. Mary had not been this interested in a long time. "And of course there's the old man from Cabanas that I never met, but hearing of his losing a big marlin to sharks gives that phantom fisherman a part." He paused and bit his lip. "But if St. Peter looked me in the eye and commanded me to give one name, just one, God help me I would give him mine ... I would give him mine because no one can give to me what I feel when I fish ... not Gregorio, not the phantom, not Carlos, not even Anselmo or Marcos ... but yours truly, my dear, yours truly." He finished his whiskey and she started to say something until he held up his hands in capitulation. "I won't get another," he surrendered. "I would like to talk about what I have in mind for the morning." He expected a response but got none. "I was thinking about doing a piece on Ernest Walsh. Remember at the Ritz when I told Charley and Hotch that nothing is as obnoxious as other people's luck? Well if I would've been really truthful, I would've added 'talent'. Well it all came home to roost when I met Ernest Walsh."

"He's no relation", she said.

"Spelled differently", he said," and besides you wouldn't want him.

"Tell me why."

"Ernest Walsh had contracted tuberculosis and spent his childhood here in Cuba. Like us, he survived a plane crash, and like me, he suffered some chronic problems. But he used his maladies to insinuate himself into other people's business; however, he did publish many expats, myself included. It was a magazine called, *This Quarter.* So by the time I had met him, he had indeed been marked for death by consumption. In fact he died in 1926 and he was only 31".

"And you wrote in your notes about him as a poseur, even though he helped you?"

"Yes."

"Didn't you just say he published a lot of your friends, including you?

"Yes."

"Well he sounds legit to me. He must've been a valuable editor."

"Yes."

"But you didn't like him at all?"

"No."

"Was it the way you didn't like Scott?

"No, that was completely different."

"Well tell me how you didn't like him."

"I met him in Ezra's studio which was just up the street from where I was living. He was with two blondes dressed in mink that he'd picked up on the ship crossing. He was dark, diseased, intense and supposedly poetic. He was talking with Ezra, I was talking with the girls."

"Of course you were."

"The blondes told me that Walsh told them he got $1200 for each poem. I knew that not to be correct."

"Did it make you jealous, his obnoxious luck or talent?"

He didn't answer the question but continued on. "Eddie Guest wrote poems at an incredible clip. He had amassed some 10 or 11,000 when he died. He was poet laureate of Michigan for God's sake."

"And you feel you should have been?"

"No, they were telling me how great Ernest Walsh was and I knew a lot of people who were a hell of a lot better than Ernest

Walsh, probably including myself."

"So you wanted them to be talking about Ernest Hemingway?"

"Maybe. But they were telling me that Walsh was making more than Eddie Guest or Rudy Kipling or anybody else for that matter."

"And that wasn't so."

"No, it wasn't so."

"And you didn't like them saying that."

"No, I didn't. Anyway they're standing there with their fancy clothes and their fancy car and their fancy boyfriend and their fancy talk and they start telling me that Ezra and I live on a poor excuse for a street and it's pitiful and my clothes were pitiful and I'd about had it. I tell them that I go to some good cafés and out to the racetracks, and they had the gall to ask me if the track would let me in with the clothes I was wearing."

"So you were upset with them?"

"Yes."

"But I bet you got their phone numbers or their room numbers."

"Yes," Ernest confessed.

"Go on, I want to hear the rest."

"Well, Walsh decides that his publication is going to award a cash prize much like *The Dial* had done. So we had lunch and he put the con on me. Back then in the notebooks, I think I described the oysters we ate is if I knew them all personally. He brought up Ezra and Joyce between oyster orders. Then I knew the con was coming when he ordered steaks with béarnaise and a good red wine. I was his date and he was gonna bang me before it was over. I felt like one of Pascin's models. Then he told me that I was going to get the prize, and not long after that he told Joyce the same thing. So now both Joyce and I think we're going to win the same prize. Ernest Walsh was a real shit. Don't you think so?" He looked at Mary. She was having trouble staying awake.

"Ezra had had discussions about Walsh with other expat artists at the time. All the usual suspects had weighed in. It was virtually unanimous. Walsh was a phony, and all but the kindest could find no redeeming values in the Irishman. And from Joyce, that was impeachment. I remembered discussing Walsh with some literary friends of friends who I had halfheartedly invited to Cuba. They turned out to be knowledgeable as hell about the '20s in Paris. It was an engaging retrospective for me. After a while the discussion got around to Walsh. One of the guests was from Detroit and took Walsh's side and I took him on. I told him Walsh wasn't true, he wasn't honest. I told him that in films, writers and directors will mark characters early on in the script. They post clues for the audience. These tips whisper to you, where this character is going and what is going to happen him. Walsh was singled out for death. His dishonesty and duplicity marked him for doom. He ruined himself. He lied to both Joyce and me. He was a poseur, a pretender, an imposter. He marked himself for death and then he died. He was *papier-mâché*. If you poked your finger in him, it would've come out with just a little dust on it. He was not purposeful or sincere. The only thing earnest about him was his name. Ernest Walsh was a prostitute. His honesty died long before he did.

"This left the guests with not much to say, aphonic if you will. Guys like Gary Cooper were everything Walsh was not—honest, straightforward, truly friendly and unspoiled. Walsh had no grace under pressure. He had no grace at all. He was not the true gen. There was nothing truthful or genuine about Ernest Walsh. I looked at the guests from Michigan who seemed withdrawn. I felt like I'd punished them maybe a little too much. I wanted somehow to make it good. So I told them that Eddie Guest was a much better fellow and Michigan's poet laureate to boot. The Detroit native seemed happy."

Ernest and Mary were in Idaho for the winter of 1958-59 while he worked on his manuscript. One night after a dinner of pheasant and fish and two brandies apiece, in front of the fire and whoever else was there at the time, the vignette about Ernest Walsh resurfaced.

"Are you having issues with that story?" Mary asked.

"No, it just ghosts me now and then. It's disquieting."

"The death part, the dying of consumption?"

"Perhaps," he said. "At that time all of us had just been

through a hellish war and though death wasn't at our doorstep, it was a lot on our minds. Sometimes it was easy to see boys marked for death like in the hospitals in Italy. There were some guys that you knew were not going to make it. Those unfortunately were much too evident. But the death of cheating yourself and others—that's different—there's nothing honorable about that—some, like Walsh, make it more obvious than others.

"Papa," Mary asked tentatively after a pause, "if you pass first, do you mind if I'm not there when it happens? It scares me so." Ernest didn't love her much anymore but he knew she was tough—made from the good stuff. He'd seen her kill game, catch monster marlins, fight off illness and survive plane crashes. She was not weak or shy or afraid.

"No," he said after a pause, "I don't mind. I'll make sure you're not there." He looked out over the valley. "There's rest beyond the river," he said to himself.

MY FRIEND EVAN

They were in Idaho, but not seeing much of each other. It was an uneasy time, difficult. Idaho had started with Martha Gellhorn in room 206 of the Sun Valley Lodge, and had always been a place to hunt and fish with the local ranchers like Bud Purdy or Bert Perrine. They fished the rivers and hunted antelope in the Pahsimeroi Valley that reminded him of Spain, but those days were over, beyond him now. His future now was not roaming the wilderness but rather keeping himself together long enough to finish the book. He knew he was not doing well at all, even though some of his friends were telling him he was okay because he was writing the Paris book and they thought it was good. But he knew he had really written the book 30 years ago and he was having a devil of a time closing it out.

He had written a sketch of Fitzgerald and had not been kind. He had not viewed the lost friendship with any regret, rather he had gone after him with little mercy. He didn't think it was fun, he thought it was necessary. Many wouldn't agree. But for as much as he resented Scott, he enjoyed Evan Shipman. In his introduction to *Men at War,* Ernest describes Shipman as one of his oldest friends and one of the bravest men he knew. In the trunks rescued at the Paris Ritz, along with the notebooks and other souvenirs from the Jazz age, there was a collection of letters. Some were from this old friend from the Paris days. He had saved later ones as well.

Evan Shipman was born in 1904 in New Hampshire. His father was a playwright and for a short time edited *Life* magazine in the early '20s. Evan went to two prep schools but finished at neither. He was, like Hemingway, close to his father and at odds with his mother. He met Ernest in Paris in 1924. He was looking for a young American named Gorham Munson who edited a small magazine and Shipman hoped to interest him in some of his poetry. When he knocked on the door of the address he had been given, he found the Hemingways on the second floor above the saw mill at 113 rue Notre Dame des Champs. Hadley described the two men's friendship as instantaneous and remarkably strong, Ernest and Evan spending two hours talking at this first meeting. Evan's experiences were not unlike those of his new friend and, above all, Ernest admired Evan's courage. Shipman found himself in the middle of one of the fiercest battles of the Spanish Civil War. Ernest saw him several months after the battle, he had been hit in both legs by machine gun bullets from a strafing plane.

"Why Hem it was absolutely nothing. It was nothing at all. I never felt a thing."

"What do you mean, you didn't feel a thing?" Ernest asked.

"While it was really nothing. You see, I was unconscious at the time."

"Yes?"

"You see the planes had just caught us in the open and bombed us and I was unconscious at the time. So I didn't feel a thing when they came down and machine gunned us. Really, Hem, it was absolutely nothing. I've hardly thought of it as a wound. It was almost like having an anesthetic beforehand."

Clearly Ernest was proud of his friend's bravery and was astonished at his expression of gratitude.

"Hem, I can never thank you enough for having brought me over here. I was very upset that you might be worried about me. I want you to know that being in Spain is the happiest time I've ever had in my life."

Ernest remembered Evan as an extremely kind and gentle man who was somehow always positive. As he sat at his desk, he thought how differently the two men had managed similar situations which didn't make him feel particularly noble.

"We both survived war injuries—shrapnel in the legs. I carried mine in my change purse and showed it around if an opportunity presented and then even had some of it forged into a ring. Evan carried his in his legs and hardly ever spoke of it and made light of the incident when he did."

If his friend had an ego it was hidden deep inside. A small pang of envy touched the old man when he read part of one of Shipman's old letters:

I hoped to have work that I was proud of to tell you about. I find I care more about that than anything and my respect for what you are doing makes me ashamed of my own limitations. I suppose that the best anyone can be is a conscience or a standard in the better sense of those words and you have always seemed that to me. What I do is so small in the face of what I want and the fault lies with my own slovenliness and procrastination.

"Talk about true and good and honest and direct. I never got there but Evan did. I acted like I did, but I didn't."

He started his now familiar slide into the shadows of depression but his admiration for his friend brought him around. He reopened another letter:

I want to write poetry again but not now until I am sure of myself with prose. What I will write then will be very different than anything I have ever done. My great trouble is getting outside of myself. I was ready to write verse 10 years before I could write a line of prose and now my imagination is so far ahead of what I can say that my mind is constantly telling it stories, working on them the first thing when I wake up or when I am walking. They are sure and complete in my mind. Only with the greatest difficulty do I ever recapture that on paper. You were right years ago, it is the most absorbing thing in the world, the hardest, the cruelest and the most fun, when it doesn't beat you by shaming you or lying to you.

"Here's somebody who really cared for me," Ernest thought sitting in Ketchum in the late fall of 1959 and looking back some 30 years:

Never asked for so much as a sou and bought me drinks at the Lilas when he couldn't afford one for himself. I wish there'd been more Evan Shipman in Ernest Hemingway.

The line about having great difficulty capturing ideas on paper hit way too close to home. For more than a year now Ernest had been lumbering through the quagmire of putting ideas to paper. It wasn't the same. It wasn't nearly the same. It was as if that ability had abandoned him and; if and when it happened to reappear, his memory would short out and erase the thought. So he was actually amazed that he remembered saying the words in the sentence he had just read. "Writing is the most absorbing thing and it is hard and cruel and enjoyable if it doesn't shame you or lie to you." It was a good sentence and it was still true. Then he read one other letter from June 1944. A friend of theirs from the expat days, Andre Masson, had just released an edition of his drawings and the artist and Shipman had met for dinner in New York. Evan had sent Ernest a copy. Andre was failing, not near what he used to be:

I liked the drawings and I wish that you would like them too… Andre is a little subdued, in fact the fierce quality that I remember so well is either gone or else buried too deep for me to have rediscovered in so short a time with him but the delicacy and the perception both about writing and painting was still there and still delightful.

Ernest thought that he had become the Andre Masson of 1944. He still had decent perception but the fight was buried deep or gone altogether. Masson, too, had both physical and psychological problems. The similarities were unsettling.

"Well," he thought, "it's time to organize a chapter around Evan. At one time, not long ago, I could've written it from memory but at least I have my Lilas notes and these letters to make it work."

In fact in one of his letters to Shipman, Hemingway had written, "I am always proud of you Evan … I'm going to write a story about you sometime to show you what I mean." This was the time. This was the place.

OPIUM

"It's hard to believe I paid $12,500 for this place. I spend that on trips now. Best thing Martha ever did, except this tower, which was Mary's idea. A writer's workshop she calls it. But I rarely come up here. It really belongs to the cats now. The bedroom is my favorite place to write, it's much more comfortable. But the view from this tower," he stopped to catch his breath," is worth the climb."

"Here in Cuba I don't know any crazy people," he thought climbing the steps, "at least in the clinical sense. Oh, there's the youngster at La Terraza who's a little sluggish and then some of the white coats are telling me I could be angling in that direction, but no—there really aren't any who are really unbalanced. Not so in Jazz age Paris. Ezra, one of my favorites, was put in Saint Elizabeth's in DC following his arraignment on treason charges. They appointed Dorothy as his legal guardian. He was in a tough place. He was declared insane, which ironically was a good thing since it saved him from a lot of jail time—maybe a life's worth. He was hospitalized for the next 12 years. In short, Ezra was crazy. And then there was his friend.

"Ralph Cheever Dunning had more than a mysterious personality, Ralph Cheever Dunning was deranged, crazier than a sprayed roach. His condition was exacerbated, if not caused, by an opium addiction. Ezra, thinking he was being the friend, supplied Dunning with what were his necessities in 1926, food and opium—not necessarily in that order. But the latter outperformed the former and Dunning would literally forget to eat. Evidently he forgot to eat quite often because he died of starvation and tuberculosis in 1930. Ezra embroiled me in his and Dunning's strange entanglement. I should've known it would be an aberrant mission, as they were both certifiable. The thing with poor Dunning was, you never knew what he would do next. I found that out the hard way."

Ezra Pound lived, in less than adequate housing, at 70 Notre Dame des Champs with his wife Dorothy who found the winters harsh and worried about her husband's health. Once when a dinner guest tried to stab him, the Pounds decided they had seen enough of Paris. Ernest held them both in high regard. He praised Ezra for coming to the defense of his friends, for getting them into print and out of trouble, paying their bills and talking them out of suicide. Ernest did, however, worry about his friend's darker side. Ezra was a fascist and was jailed for being a traitor. So he moved to Italy in 1924. He had a voracious sexual appetite. They were lined up for him: Hilda Doolittle, Viola Baxter, Mary Moore, Margaret Cravens, Olga Rudge. Dorothy and Olga bore him children.

"He was a one-man scandal sheet," Ernest had told Hotch. "I always wanted to write a short piece on his time as a teacher in Crawfordsville, Indiana. That Midwest town was about as reactionary, conservative and rigid as Ezra was revolutionary, liberal and reckless. He did everything he could to drive the administration crazy. It would've made good reading. It might have been as stimulating as the opium he wanted to leave with me when he left for Italy in 1924. He wanted me to hold it and medicate Ralph Dunning when he needed it. He neglected, however, to tell me how I would divine when that was. Dunning was a poet, and opium smoker and caretaker of one of the strangest personalities in Paris at the time. He wrote but he didn't care what happened to it after he wrote it. He didn't talk much, as far as I knew, Ezra was one of the few people who could actually engage him in a conversation. However, before his death at age 50, he did win a very nice poetry prize. He would smoke opium and not eat. He was a mess. He was dying just before Ezra was to leave town. Lying there, near Ezra's studio, he looked like he had already died. He was marked for death with an indelible mark. Ezra, kind man that he was, stood for his bills. I was in charge of the opium, an employment for which I had absolutely no training and even less inclination. My first test came when Dunning had managed, against all odds, to attain the roof of the studio and would not dismount. Ezra had told me I was to deliver the goods in an emergency. If this wasn't an emergency, what was? So I grabbed the opium jar and headed out in search of my patient. I found him, he had come down from the roof but he looked desperate. He had that hundred yard, blank stare in his eyes. I handed him the jar with Ezra's regards. I had concluded early on that by mentioning Ezra in any conversation I would be on safer ground. Not so much on this occasion. He took the jar from my hand, checked it out and then threw it at me like a catcher going to second base. Just about the time the jar hit me, all the swear words he could think of were hitting me as well. He really swore at me professionally and if that wasn't quite enough he tossed a milk bottle that found its mark and then, building on his success, threw two others. Milk bottle shrapnel was flying all over the place.

"It was one of the few times when I had legitimately tried to come to someone's aid and barely escaped. Ezra was convinced that Dunning was a worthwhile poet. Evan Shipman couldn't decide if the entire situation was a comedy or a mystery and I wondered whether Dunning thought I might have been part of the local law enforcement. Whatever the situation, Dunning had a good arm and enviable accuracy. He had been born in Detroit and seemed to be devoid of both ambition and common sense. He did die of tuberculosis and malnourishment much too early. It was interesting that he wrote in a poetic form called terza-rima which is a three line system of rhyming used by Dante.

MR JAZZ AGE

Ernest and Mary were in their Idaho kitchen, having just finished lunch and resting. They had been engaged in conversation most of the morning. He had been unable to write. He had tried. He wrote a few of his true sentences, consulted the transcriptions but couldn't keep it going. It made him mad. He was angry for 10 minutes or so and then it depressed him for five minutes or so and then it frightened him for a long time. He needed help but he was convinced there was nowhere to get it.

"Maybe if I take a short walk, it'll help get me started.," he thought, desperation edging in. But then Mary, no longer in love with him, but still his friend, still capable of pity, engaged him in prosaic conversation to even his keel. It worked, he changed focus which was no longer an easy feat. "Maybe," she thought, "if I talk him back to something in his journals, I can get him started again."

"Could I ask you some questions Papa, questions about the past?"

"That covers a lot of territory," he said straight-faced.

"Yes, but I won't ask that many."

"Okay, if I get tired, I might have to rest."

"Fair enough," she said, "the deal is made." She hesitated.

"Go ahead," he said with a hint of anticipation.

"What was your most difficult relationship?" She knew she was entering a danger zone. His life had been a minefield of risky relationships starting with his mother. And the last thing she wanted to hear again was what a wonderful wife Hadley had been. But she doubted Hadley, remembered by Ernest as his first and best attempt at marriage, would be the most difficult relationship. Pauline, perhaps—Martha, maybe—surely present company would be excluded. Ernest had been thinking for a minute. He surprised her with the answer.

"Scott," was all he said. The longer she thought about it, the more sense it made."We were the best of friends and the best of enemies. We were both good at what we did and held the limelight for quite some time. When it was all said and done, I was certain I had the edge but damn the *Gatsby* was incredibly good and to have named the Jazz Age certainly put him on the map for good."

"But that all pales to the Pulitzer and the Nobel," she noted. He kept on as if he hadn't heard her.

"Our relationship was dysfunctional at best. He took a few shots at me and they were artfully aimed. The remark about me giving a helping hand to a man on a ledge above me. That did not make me feel too wonderful in fact I was bitter for a long time, in fact I'm still bitter. Jealousy is a grotesque beast and I was one. He had been good to me. I was a shit to him and I've been blamed by many for sabotaging the friendship. But Scott sabotaged himself with alcohol and bad behavior. We parted ways in 1926 and only crossed paths a few times over the next 10 years or so. I owe him, but I owe him." Mary didn't understand that last remark but she let it go. "Kitten," he said nodding his head, "you've got me thinking. I think I can put a few hundred words together on Scott. Lord knows I've got enough café notes for a chapter or two or maybe more."

The chapter on Scott Fitzgerald could have been the most difficult for Ernest. The opening three sentences are beautifully written. They disclose the legendary two sides of Scott. The young, bright spectacularly literate storyteller leading the parade of expats and then the not so sober, often morose, struggling older version. Fitzgerald soared past all the men of his own generation and then became victim to an incredibly toxic mix of personal demons. Ernest worked on the chapter in Cuba and then packed up the Paris book when they went to Idaho in 1959.

From the quiet house overlooking the river, Mary—who wasn't keen on hearing any more about Hadley—or any of the others for that matter—didn't ask too many questions about Paris; but the chapters on Scott and Zelda fascinated her.

"Can you tell me about you and the Fitzgeralds?"

"I watched it all unfold," said Ernest looking out the window down to the river. "I watched him touch the sun with *Gatsby*. It was 1924 and I was still poor as dirt and he was in some ways living like Gatsby. He and Zelda were the toast of every town I knew. They were the lobby posters for the real-life film of the roaring '20s, the Jazz age—for God's sake he even invented the term. They were also the roar in the roaring, and he had been kind to me, in several ways, connections, money, praise, friendships. Was I jealous? What do you think? They were a handsome couple with wealth and manners and going at top speed. Hell yes I was—though I wouldn't let myself believe it. I knew that it would cripple me if I let it."

"How did it end up with Scott—did you see him much after Paris?"

"As you know I traveled a lot and so did he, but to different places and once Zelda was sick, our paths were strangers and so were we.

"When was Zelda hospitalized?" Mary asked.

"I'm pretty sure it was 1930—she was a schizophrenic. She was at a sanitarium in France then Switzerland."

"And you and Zelda didn't get along."

"We hated each other. But I did feel sorry for her, she was sick a long time. She was sick for a long time when Scott couldn't afford for her to be sick. She died in a fire in the spring of 1948 at the hospital where she was being treated."

"But you liked Scott well enough, didn't you. I know you did, you told me you did."

"Yes," he said after hesitating, "but that too was complicated."

"But you knew he was great at what he did—especially in the beginning?"

"Yes," he said this time with no hesitation, "I did know that and when he finished *Gatsby* and I read it, I loved him for writing it and how good I knew it was but I didn't like that I didn't have something that good that I could show him."

"You were jealous?" She asked and he didn't answer.

"It spurred me to write a novel. *Gatsby* was in 1925, Scribner's published it in April—the cruelest month according to Eliot and then to me. They published my *Torrents of Spring* the next year.

"The first paragraph of this sketch you wrote on him for your Paris book is beautiful. Would you read it to me?"

"Oh Mary ... I'm tired ... how about..."

"It's only a few sentences."

"How about you read it to me?"

"Okay," she said after a moment, "I will." And she did.

"You read well," he said when she'd finished. "And for that I'll show you something I came across not too long ago."

"What?"

"A loose piece of paper in amongst the souvenirs from the trunks."

"About the Fitzgeralds?"

"About Scott."

"Did you write it?"

"This is hard for me to say, dear girl, but I don't really remember."

"That's okay it's been a long time, is it in your handwriting?"

"It's typed."

"By Nita?"

"No I don't think so—paper's too old. Can't tell ... could've been me... it's like what you just read me."

"Okay, let me see it," she asked and he went to the varnished bookshelf and came back with a single sheet of yellowed paper.

"Will you read it to me?" He asked, handing it to her. She looked at it in silence for a moment or so.

"Sure. She hesitated. 'Effortless butterfly, with magic wings, unaware of how you flew, touched the sun, then gave away your patterned dust, and fell to earth, marked for death, your redemption lost forever.' I like it and it's too close to your paragraph to be a coincidence."

"I think I wrote it. It feels familiar. When Charley Ritz gave me these notebooks in Paris, it made me remember Scott a lot. I hadn't thought of him for a long time. But the trunks and the notebooks and Paris helped me remember him. I met him in April, 1925 in the Dingo bar. He had come in with a baseball pitcher from Princeton, kid named Chaplin. He was a good kid—in fact I preferred him to Scott."

"Even then?"

"Yes," anyway Scott was a good-looking man—damn near pretty, with his light hair in waves, blue eyes, strong features. He went on about what a good writer I was, it was awkward. Someone told us back then that praise to your face was an open disgrace."

"I think there are people today that would have trouble believing that."

"Meaning?"

"Meaning that if a young man at the top of the literary heap, upon meeting you, told you what a good writer you were, that you would be mad."

"Well I was. He was dressed in Brooks Brothers and had a Guard's tie with slanted stripes of dark blue and magenta. He hadn't been in the Brigade of Guards and if some Brit had walked in and asked him when he was in the Brigade, he would've been in a tight spot. But he was buying champagne which healed a lot. Scott was only 5'9", he was short."

"Papa I measured you once on the scale and you were 5'11" so he was only 2 inches shorter than you."

"I am 6 feet tall," he said in a tone which left absolutely no room for doubt.

Scott had published *This Side of Paradise,* his first novel, in 1920. The book sold out in three days. He was only 23. He was a distant cousin of Francis Scott Key who wrote the words to the national anthem during the war of 1812 and for whom he was named. Fitzgerald played on this family connection like Ernest played on the supposed 3 inch height advantage. Scott couldn't spell very well and continually misspelled Hemingway, using two m's. He did this for at least two years. He left Princeton and was a second lieutenant in the Army in 1917 but just before he was to ship out, the armistice was signed. Zelda was Miss Jazz Age. She was a beautiful and erratic flapper. She smoked, drank, cursed some and painted, danced and wrote. She was talented. They were "the couple", the toast of the '20s, but the '30s found them tragically different. Scott gave into alcohol and

Zelda had a meltdown and was institutionalized for most of the rest of her life.

"Scott and I parted ways in the late '20s. After that I was tough on him more than once in the press and elsewhere. In the late '30s Scott said we could never sit across from each other again. And I have to admit, Kitten, that when *Gatsby*—and I knew, knew it was a winner—but when it didn't sell at first, instead of feeling sorry, I smiled. Originally he had only sold about 20,000 copies. During the second war, there was an armed services edition put out that accounted for 150,000 copies being shipped overseas." Ernest fell silent.

"And?" Coaxed Mary.

"And in the late '30s he was in the soup, drunk, broke and looking for work. He desperately needed a loan. I had the wherewithal to help him but I didn't. He had helped me plenty the decade before, when he had it and I didn't. Now the tables were turned and I ignored him. I don't feel good about that. It speaks to something I'd rather not admit to myself … or you."

"It's okay, things like that happen. People fall in and out of friendships just like they fall in and out of love." The last part of that sentence was to excuse him for his first three wives in case he was feeling at this time like he needed an excuse. It was also to excuse her.

"Scott was in Hollywood. He was a script doctor and he needed a real one. He tried over and over to beat the bottle but it didn't take. He was even quoted as saying he couldn't even make the grade as a hack. And then he gave it one more, brave try. He started a novel about his experience in Hollywood."

"The Last Tycoon."

"Yes—but he was drowning in debt and booze. He told Zelda he was mining the damn thing out of himself like uranium. A month later his heart killed him. The poor bastard was 44 … never finished the novel. The critics thought he was really on to something with that last book but some of that had to be the sympathy vote."

It was a soft winter afternoon the next day. Ernest had worked some on the Paris book and Mary had been writing letters. They talked some more about the roaring '20s and the night Ernest and Scott had met.

"When the champagne had coated us with a warm fog, Scott's skin seemed to stretch over his face until his head was close to being just the skull. It was like a drunken death mask. Everything drew tighter, lips, cheeks, his eyes receded and he grew very pale and resembled the wax figures in the Tussaud Museum. Scott's death mask which would come much too early anyway, made an even more premature appearance that night. I asked him if he was okay but he didn't answer. Chaplin, his Princeton baseball buddy, said he'd be okay, that he'd seen alcohol take him like this before. I saw him at the Lilas not long after and he acted like nothing had happened. He was false about it."

"So Scott was one of your favorites at the Lilas?"

"Not so much, but we did have a long talk, that evening not long after I saw his death mask."

"About what?"

"More like about whom."

"Okay, whom?" She grinned.

"George Lorimer."

"The editor of the *Post*?"

"Yes—he published 50 or 60 of Scott's short stories. Then Scott asked me to read *Gatsby*. He said he'd get me his copy and was not conceited at all and I couldn't wait to read it. It was strange because the critics loved it but sales were not good initially. He showed me a review by Gilbert Seldes who edited *The Dial*. He was a real fan of *Gatsby* and Scott. The best thing was that Scott did not develop a death mask that night. I still thought that drink had marked him for death but at the Lilas he was good. He did not act up as he had at the Dingo. In fact he was a perfect gentleman. He always had great manners and that evening on the terrace of the Lilas he was charming as hell."

"Wasn't that the meeting you told me about, the story of Zelda and the Rennie being left in Lyon and your trip with Scott to pick it up?"

"The very one. We planned to take the fast train in the morning, only one stop and then Lyon. The plan was for us to arrive, get the car serviced, have a literary dinner and get an early jump back to Paris the next morning. It sounded to me like it could be fun. I was looking forward to the trip. Quality time with a famous writer that I didn't need Miss Stein to arrange. I had known Scott only as a short story writer for the *Saturday Evening Post*, but when he told me how he changed the stories so they would sell to the magazine, I thought he was whoring. He said he had to do it to make money from the magazines to buy the time to write novels. I didn't agree with that method but I couldn't argue too loudly or too long as I had yet to publish a novel and I couldn't imagine doing so as it took me half a day to write a paragraph. So we're all set with a plan to pick up the Renault in Lyon. By the way, I have somewhere a picture of that old car with him and Zelda and little Scotty. It's a nice photo and they all look happy and well. Going to Lyon, which was a bit of a trip, some 300+ miles and a good part of the day, made me wish I had my own car but that was a lot of money back then and we had a stipend of $3000 a year from Hadley and I was not knocking them dead yet. I had an advance on the short story book and had sold a few stories to the Germans and the Review but we were living on the margin, saving our money to travel to ski or go to Spain for the festivals.

"What about the trip, that's the best part of the story?"

"Good Lord woman, you're as impatient as I used to be."

"What do you mean, used to be?" And she kicked her fur slipper at him.

"We were going to leave from Gare d Lyon—scene of the lost manuscripts," he still winced but the regret had long faded, "and I was there waiting for his eminence. He had the tickets but he didn't show, at least I hadn't seen him show. So I bought a ticket of my own—not first-class like Scott probably had—but a ticket nonetheless and railed to Lyon. I should have known this trip was marked for deep water. Pretty soon it was noon and I was hungry, it seemed I was always hungry, and I had to spend money—that I watched like a hawk — on lunch and a bottle of wine. I was annoyed and I would be more so, shortly. I made calls to his place in Paris. He had left but the maid didn't know where he was staying so I checked expensive hotels in Lyon but no dice so I went where? He looked at Mary.

"To a café perhaps?"

"Aren't you clever," and he kicked her slipper back to her. "Yes, I went to a café for a drink and to read the newspaper. There I met a real character, a performer who did strange things. He was a fire eater and bent francs in his mouth. He was hungry having eaten not much more than fire, so I bought us both dinner at an inexpensive Algerian place with a decent wine. We had lamb. The only reason I can remember that, is that every time I go to an Algerian restaurant that's what I order. I told him I wrote stories and he said he could put me next to some terrific stories in North Africa. We said goodbye and I went to the hotel. Still no word from Scott, who was now Fitzgerald to me. I went to sleep while reading one of the Russians I had brought with me from Sylvia's. The next morning he finally made it and apologized. Zelda wasn't well and he was fearful he should've stayed in Paris to look after her. Unfortunately he would get a lot of practice doing that. We had a large and long breakfast and had to wait while the hotel packed us a lunch that cost as much as the Ritz. We had a drink while we waited. I remember paying for the hotel and the drink although he offered to pay for it all. I knew there were places I could borrow money back in Paris. Well, we picked up the car and of all things it had no top. Evidently it had been damaged and Zelda didn't want it replaced. He said she did not favor tops on cars. I had no raincoat and it rained about an hour north of Lyon and then about nine or 10 other times. We spent a lot of time seeking shelter and I must say the expensive lunch lived up to its price. We drank the wine they had packed and I bought four more on the way."

"Was that smart Papa?"

"But it was good wine," he said with a grin.

"Scott was worried about his health and that was a topic for many miles. I told him that a good white wine was good medicine. Then it rained heavily, so we stopped and where did we go?"

"The next café?"

"Right again Kitten. Then we took a hotel for the evening. Our clothes were soaked and Scott was very worried about a disease he thought he had, but he looked okay. He was going through a period of self-diagnosis. It was like fellows I knew who had graduated from medical school. Every time they studied a disease they thought they had it. Anyway he thought he was sick but he didn't seem to have a fever and his lungs sounded clear and his pulse was 72. He had no symptoms that would indicate that he was anything but healthy. I told him he was fine and to have a lemonade and whiskey—which my father had called a toddy—and take an aspirin. He was convinced he had congestion of the lungs and nothing I told him made any difference. He wanted a thermometer to make sure he didn't have a fever. My feeling his forehead wasn't good enough. I paid a waiter to get a thermometer and some whiskeys."

"So Scott Fitzgerald was a hypochondriac?"

"Definitely with a capital H and he was also a champion at self-diagnosis. He was worried about lung congestion because he heard alcoholism worked its way to that eventually and, sure enough, it took him although his heart gave out before his lungs did. The waiter came with the whiskeys and aspirin and lemon juice but no thermometer because the pharmacy had closed. Scott denigrated the waiter to some extent and I thought of Evan Shipman and Jean in the Lilas and the good friends we all were. Not so with Scott, at that time Scott was not a fan of the French or the Italians. After the whiskeys I thought things would be better, but that was not to be. He wanted his temperature taken, he wanted his clothes dried, he wanted to get on a train and go to a hospital. Finally the waiter came back but with a bath thermometer mounted on a piece of wood. It was not small. Scott looked at it. His eyes were wider than they'd been for days.' Where does that thing go?' He asked half panicked. 'Not there,' I reassured. I told him it went under his arm. He relaxed. I put it under his arm and left it there for three or four minutes. It read 37 something. It was centigrade. I told him it was normal but I had no idea. He wanted me to take mine to compare. I did and it was the same as his. It would've been the same for anyone because the thermometer did not move. He wanted to call Zelda. He told me it was the first night they had not been together. We had more whiskeys and Scott told me a lot about Zelda and himself including the affair she had on the Riviera with a French naval aviator. Maybe that was why he didn't like the French. Scott could tell a story. Listening to him was easier than reading his misspelled, miss punctuated letters. He misspelled my name for two years. Finally our dry clothes came and we went to dinner. We had drinks and he passed out quietly with his head on his arms."

Ernest kept on with Mary, she asking enough questions to keep the narrative alive—he enjoying the memories both from the '20s and from reconstituting them now. Mary could tell that alcohol had been at the center of his life for a long time. He spoke about drinking many whiskeys and bottles of wine and more whiskeys and more wine as if it were *de rigueur*. Whatever other maladies Scott had or Ernest was having, alcohol certainly wouldn't help them. Mary had a friend who had medical issues that he survived and his physician credited the fact he never drank for his success. She was afraid Ernest would pay the price. She had looked at the Paris book and noticed the prominence of drinking. He insisted that his training for writing was never to drink after dinner or before he wrote or while writing. But she knew that wasn't so. He had penned the famous line, "Write drunk, edit sober."

"The next day," he continued, "we drove to Paris and he told me everything I would ever need to know about Michael Arlen who he described as an Armenian dandy whose real name was unpronounceable, who married a countess, who drove her yellow Rolls and who wrote a good book. He also said he had exquisite manners ... faultless manners were always important to Scott. On the way back when we stopped, I ordered wine and asked him not to let me order anymore. He gave me some of his when he saw me worrying that mine was about gone. We drove to his place on rue Tilsitt in Paris and I took a taxi to the sawmill, it was good to be home and I went to the Lilas for a drink and vowed never to go on a trip with anyone I didn't love. It would take love to counteract all the troubles that haunt expeditions. I saw Scott in a few days when he brought *Gatsby* over. I was impressed that he had remembered but put off somewhat with the dust jacket art. I took it off when I read the book. When I finished it, I knew I wanted to be his friend. The book was very fine and I had not yet met Zelda. She was like my iceberg premise, she was not there but she was getting a lot of attention."

MRS JAZZ AGE

In January 1959, Hemingway's friend Gary Cooper visited him in Idaho and they went bird hunting at Silver Creek, near Picabo. Silver Creek is a tributary of the Little Wood River. There were plenty of trout as well as birds. It must have reminded Ernest of Michigan. He and "Coops" had been friends for 20 years, they had an extraordinary, if unlikely, friendship that would be the subject of a feature length documentary 50 years later. They both loved the outdoors. Bud Purdy was a local rancher who hunted and fished with Ernest. Others in the Idaho crew were Lloyd and Tillie Arnold, Don Anderson, Duke MacMullen and George Saviers.

January in his home, at 400 Canyon Run Boulevard on 17 acres on the outskirts of Ketchum on the banks of the Big Wood River, was comfortable. The house, designed to resemble the Sun Valley Lodge, was decorated, as was the Finca, with bullfight souvenirs. He had started coming to the Wood River Valley in the late 30s, staying in the Sun Valley Lodge. He wrote *For Whom the Bell Tolls* there in a room he shared with Martha Gellhorn. Not till 1959 did he and Mary purchase "Topping House" for $50,000. There was a breakfast of poached eggs on toast and strong mountain coffee. He ate all of it and was upstairs walking out of the mint green bathroom. There were some remnants of coals from last night's fire in the outsized fieldstone fireplace. He added two small cottonwood logs hoping they would ignite as he planned to work at the Cuban made desk and chair. The transcribed chapters and his moveable Paris book manuscript were there on the desk. Several nights ago he had dreamt that he had lost the manuscript. He had wakened in a sweat. It was the lost valise all over again. Hadley at the Gare de Lyon and the manuscripts gone missing. But there they were stacked on his desk. This morning he would work. It did not come easy. Others, Mary, Kotch, even visitors noticed the struggle and he was slowly admitting to it. His blood pressure was high and his morale was low. He had liver disease, diabetes and arteriosclerosis. His condition was not good nor was his prognosis. But this morning he would work. He would weave a tale from his café notes. He sat down and opened to an antique ribbon bookmark he kept in the Paris book. He had not lost track of his sketches but he was losing track of himself. He looked out the window and through the trees. A hawk circled above. Perhaps it was a sign. He would write a chapter about Zelda.

Like Miss Stein and Alice whose gravitas took more than one chapter, so too does Mr. Fitzgerald and Zelda. Perhaps it is not a coincidence that this foursome, once good friends, fell out of favor with Ernest and left a familiar shaped void in his future.

"Mary, you're not jealous of my work are you?" He asked more tentatively than not. Years ago he wouldn't have even entertained the thought.

"Of course not—I'm surprised you asked. I love your work," thinking she loved his work more than she loved him.

"Well Zelda was jealous of Scott's."

"Yes but didn't he borrow a lot of her life for his novels?"

"I think that's fair to say, but she undercut his efforts with great regularity. In *Gatsby* he wrote about parties where people would go off like rockets and if it were raining, and someone wanted it to stop, they merely paid someone. Scott and Zelda went to parties like that. They threw parties like that. Zelda got used to parties like that and when Scott was writing she would get bored and drag him off to another drunken party."

"Are you sure there was a lot of dragging involved?"

"I'm sure the drinking was an attraction, probably by then a magnetism from which he could not escape. He would destroy himself and they would quarrel and makeup and then he and I would take long walks and he would sweat out the drink. Then he would start to write again and the passion play would repeat.

To his credit he loved her completely and was jealous as hell of her. Her affair with Jozan the fly boy damn near did him in. Zelda had asked for a divorce. He locked her in the house until she relented. Later they acted like none of it had ever happened. But not long after, she overdosed on pills. All this was while he was writing *Gatsby*. Both of them would drink till they passed out, which offered an excuse to cover many episodes. He had written the best American novel I had ever read and it wasn't paying him so he was writing stories for the magazines. It really bothered me that he would adapt them for publication. He wasn't being true to himself or the story. He wasn't writing it straight. She was jealous of his work and seemed to do all she could to keep him from writing. During that summer in Spain, mainly because he had written *Gatsby*, I started *Torrents of Spring* which I finished back in Paris. He and Zelda had been on the Riviera and when I saw him this time he was drunk too much of the time, day and night. He did manage to start another novel, but he would visit me when he was drinking and interrupt my work much like Zelda did his. But when he was sober he was a very good friend."

"What year was this?"

"Well in '25 he was upset that I wouldn't show him the first draft of *The Sun Also Rises*, the title then was *Fiesta*. It was not yet finished. It needed rewriting. It was about then that Zelda had a stomach condition. They invited us down to the Riviera in June. He was writing again and Zelda had taken up painting. He was making money on *Gatsby*. Zelda looked terrific, summer beautiful, and her hawk's eyes were clear and calm. There is a water color self-portrait that shows her hawk's eyes very clearly. At a welcoming party for us, she told me she had a secret. She asked me if I thought Al Jolson was greater than Jesus. Now there's one you don't catch every day. I've been asked some strange questions in a lot of places, in a number of languages, but none like that. It was then that I knew she was in deep trouble. Zelda's mother had been an aspiring actress and Zelda had those genes, she wanted to be out front, she wanted to be the center of attention, she wanted to do crazy things. But in that June of 1926 when she asked me about Mr. Jolson, I knew she wasn't right and I told Scott. He knew I hadn't liked her before I met her and blamed my diagnosis on that. But she was slipping off the cliff as history proved. If you looked in her eyes you could see her mind leave from time to time. "

"Can you see mine leave?"

"Sometimes at night," he said and threw her a kiss with his lips, thinking it had been a very long time since the two had kissed. "There was an incident in a very fancy restaurant, I believe it was the *Colombe d'Or*, a very upscale restaurant in *Saint-Paul-de-Vence*. Zelda was very mad at Scott who was on his knee talking to a very old Isadora Duncan—she died, I think, the next year when her big red silk scarf tangled in the wheel of a convertible Amilcar—but anyway by then she had faded and had purple hair. But she had lived across the street from the Dingo bar, where Scott and I had met, and had known him for a long time. It was Scott and an old friend having a chat. In short she was no one to inspire jealousy. Anyway Zelda was so upset that she jumped down a staircase and banged herself up. I've been in that restaurant and have seen that staircase, it is made of stone and she's lucky she didn't kill herself. There was also a time she tossed an incredibly expensive engagement present watch Scott had given her out of the train window because of an imagined affair between Scott and a young actress named Lois Moran.

SIZE MATTERS

Ernest felt poorly most of the time and was a significant source of worry for his friend Duke MacMullen, who watched over him closely when they walked Silver Creek. He would constantly dissuade the old hunter from taking a shotgun out for any reason. The author spent more and more time indoors and while still in Ketchum in the winter of 1958-59, he managed to finish his vendetta with Scott.

The last third of the Fitzgerald trilogy deals with Scott's anatomy. Evidently Ernest and Scott had gone to lunch at Michaud's which had become known in their circle as James Joyce's place. Scott said he had a very important question that he needed answered with absolute honesty and he thought he could trust Ernest to do that. It was a most personal question. The story seems a bit too fanciful, but they did have a strange relationship.

"Here's one for you Mary—Zelda had asked me about Al Jolson, Scott asked me about his manhood." Mary just laughed.

"I was wondering if he was walking down the same path as his wife. I thought he was losing it. We had talked about writing and friends and other subjects that were definitely prelims to the main event. And then he asked it, after dessert, the question to which he needed the absolute truth: He told me that Zelda told him, because of the way he was built, he could never make any woman happy. We went to the gents, I checked his equipment and told him he was fine. He still wanted proof. I told him to compare the statues in the Louvre with his in the mirror so that he would be judging from the same angle. I couldn't believe we were going from the loo to the Louvre. Scott was 5'9" and he was in proportion. He asked me why Zelda would tell him that and I explained that it was intended to keep him from straying. She had worried about Isadora, she had worried about Lois Moran—she didn't want to worry anymore and the way of doing that was to make him believe he couldn't satisfy any of them, that he would only embarrass himself. So I took him to the Louvre and we sized up some statues."

"What a reason to visit the museum, but it's probably just as well you weren't in Florence looking at David."

"They should've added it to their brochure. I didn't stop there, I gave him the tutorial. It was hardly the Kama Sutra but I did give him tips on angles and the use of pillows and positions. He listened intently. I was just hoping I wouldn't wind up in a short story or novel.

"Years later after the Second World War, Georges the bar chief at the Ritz, but back then he was just starting off in the '20s, asked me who Scott Fitzgerald was. I told him. He told me he did not remember Scott but he did remember Baron von Blixen-Finecke who was a Swedish writer and African big-game hunter. He married Karen Dinesen in Kenya and they ran a coffee plantation. He also ran a firm of Safari guides. He died in Sweden from injuries sustained in a car crash. He was also an accomplished writer. His first wife, Karen, wrote *Out Of Africa* which was a favorite of mine. You would've thought that Georges would've remembered a writer like Fitzgerald who was so much better and more famous than the Baron."

"Yes, wouldn't you," she said sensing the acrimony still residing in her husband of 23 years, who lately had been showing signs of remorse for his expat antics.

PARIS AND PAULINE

He wanted to write a final, leave-taking chapter about how Paris never ends, how it stays with you forever. His notebooks, of course, were a profusion of Paris. They were a diagnosis of the city, an exploration, inspection, and investigation. Paris had been the backdrop, the permanent stage scenery, for the characters who starred in the other chapters. This chapter would be about his goodbye to Paris and to the wife who had helped make it the extraordinary experience it was.

He would once again start with the winter weather that would chase them to Austria for the ski season, setting the stage for the circumstances that led to his first venture into what would become an overlapping monogamy—a staggered polygamy. He would think of it as bad luck, having two women to love.

His buckeye and rabbit foot would desert and disappoint. Perhaps his failure to knock on wood had led him astray. Maybe the pilot fish had performed his task too well and the unmarried young woman—the temporary best friend—proved much more than clever when she moved in with the family of three and made it a family of one. And for someone who routinely lamented his poverty, a woman of serious wealth might have held great attraction.

The home in Key West, the apartment in Paris, the first two cars, the safari were all gifts from her family—mostly her Uncle Gus who gifted them money throughout their marriage. But when all was said and done, this chapter was a wave from a moving window to the city he loved and which loved him back … a tribute to the amaranthine quality of Paris and all that made it so never ending.

"It was cold in Paris in the winter and Hadley did not think it was habitable and it was also too much for Bumby—so we went to Austria, the town of Schruns, the hotel Taube. It was a great place for skiing and glacier hiking. I learned to ski there."

"It was too cold in Paris, so you went to the snow in Austria?" Mary asked just to stir the pot.

"We went to a winter resort which Paris is not. This was a cold to enjoy, not a damp, dark cold that interfered. It was a vacation. Bumby went in his little sleigh. There were no ski lifts then, anything you skied down you had to climb back up. It made you fit, we loved skiing, on glaciers or deep powder."

"But you are spending too much time on skiing in a sketch about Paris." There was nothing constructive about her criticism.

"Perhaps I'll change the title," he snapped defensively.

"There is never an end to winter?" she suggested. After she said it she thought it was mean spirited. He shook his head and started to get up. "I'm sorry," she said, "that was uncalled for." After a short pause he continued reading.

"And of course there was eating and drinking, light beer, dark beer, red wine, white wine, kirsch, schnapps. And for reading we had books from Sylvia's and there was bowling and even poker though it was *verboten.* Our rooms were warmed by those painted porcelain stoves that were really pieces of art, and the burning wood had an agreeable scent. There would be big breakfast feasts, fresh bread and fruit preserves, eggs, ham and coffee. There was a big dog that adopted us and I would ski down with him on my back and he was Bumby's friend for the season."

"Were you able to work there?"

"Yes and very well. There was not the relaxed comfort of here with a Gulfstream or the warm night walks. But in the winter of '25-'26, I worked well on the *Sun Also Rises,* settled on the biblical title from *Ecclesiastes* which is a message of hope, and I finished the novel and several stories. I accomplished quite a bit, and we met many friendly Alpine people who skied and drank with us and then went home and spun their own wool and knitted sweaters. The wool was natural and the fat had not been removed, so when you wore one and it rained you could smell the lanolin.

"But not everything was Alpine wonder. There was an awkward night when some German naval officer made a scene about John Jellicoe of the British Admiralty who commanded his fleet against the Germans in Jutland in 1916. It was a huge naval battle off the coast of Denmark with over 200 ships and 100,000 men and both sides claimed victory but England kept control of the North Sea. The officer was a jerk, he upset everyone, especially the Germans—they were embarrassed.

"And then it turned out that this winter was the year of all the avalanches. The conditions were ripe for trouble; snow came late and the slopes were warm from the sun when serious snow fell but it was not bound to the earth. There were some Berliners who insisted on skiing even though they were warned not to. There were 13 of them, and nine died. Others died that year as well—it was not a good ski season."

"Is that when you grew your beard," Mary asked to keep the story alive. It seemed lately that the more he talked the less he slid into depression and the fewer black ass days he would have.

"Yes and I let my hair grow. It was easier, warmer and it hid my face from the sun, and the sun bouncing off the snow. The villagers called me the Black Christ—which is a hell of a title to live up to. And besides the avalanches there were whiteouts when you couldn't see 10 feet. It was like a white bowl from the kitchen had been placed over you. But the next year was even worse."

"Why, what happened then?"

"The rich people arrived, with their pilot fish."

"Pilot fish?"

"You know, the smaller fish that follow large fish like sharks and rays, and eat small parasites that are attached to the larger fish, and leftovers from the larger fish's meals."

"So they are parasites that eat smaller parasites."

"You could say."

"What is a pilot fish out of the water?"

"Someone who congregates around rich people and basically kisses their ass."

"Anyone I know?"

"Dos Passos and the Murphys."

"Really?" As she spoke she was thinking Dos was still alive and would be an unnamed pilot fish and Sarah and Gerald would be anonymous as well.

"Yes. He brought them in, enough of them to mess up our situation and then he left … left us holding the sharkskin bag. The year before they would not have come. But now we were doing well, a novel had been written, and stories, and the Black Christ was here and there was something, I guess, to see. The pilot fish had set them up. He was our friend and their friend and he could lead them to us and he guided them in and they insinuated themselves into our well-being, infiltrated our lives. I did not like myself when I was around these piloted rich. I actually sat there and read part of my new novel like a damned trained dog.

"Then Pauline came. Piloted right to me like a shark. Pauline came with a plan. She came with a plan to sink every tooth she had into me and pull me out to sea. I was writing and then all of a sudden I had two attractive girls around when I had finished work and one was new and strange. At first it is appealing and exhilarating but like all things evil and wayward and amoral—I lied; and I hated myself when I lied.

"Every day was a danger. You live day by day, you battle day by day. It's combat and you can't go on like that and, eventually, you give up."

Mary wanted to say, it doesn't sound to me as if it were all Pauline's fault or even that of the pilot fish but she didn't. She also wanted to ask what would happen if a Pauline—piloted or not—showed up here in Cuba, at the Finca, in the living room, the pool, on the *Pilar*—but she didn't think that would be wise, not that she cared about the answer.

She also wanted to know how much of this was directed at the Murphys out of jealousy, particularly at Sarah because he had wanted her for himself and couldn't have her. Maybe he also disliked her for being Nicole Diver in *Tender is the Night,* just like he disliked Mike Strater for being Burne Halliday in *This Side of Paradise.*

"It got worse. *I* got much worse. I left Schruns to go to the publisher in New York and when I got to Paris I did not catch the train to Austria. Pauline was in Paris and I was in Paris and there was trouble in Paris."

Again Mary wanted to comment but knew she shouldn't and didn't.

"When I finally got to Schruns, guilt dripping from every pore, Hadley was there and of course she looked lovely and Bumby looked lovely and I did love her and I believed it. I believed it till I got back to Paris and the battle started again. Paris would never be the same. I would never be the same, Hadley would never be the same, and worst of all, we would never be the same."

Mary looked at the broken remnant of the man she had married 14 years ago. There had been many good times, inconceivable good times, but now it was hopeless. Their marriage was in ashes. He abused her more than loved her, and at times she wasn't even sure he liked her any more. He had been a real bastard in Spain and it wasn't much better here. There were times she even feared him. She wrote him letters to avoid being with him. Listening to his Paris memoir passed for entertainment. She had even offered to move out. She couldn't go on like this.

FOR REASONS SUFFICIENT TO THE AUTHOR

For the last few days he had been markedly disoriented. The last 72 hours had been unsettling for both he and Mary as well as the household staff.

He could not write; he was bewildered, adrift, sluggish and sometimes utterly lost.

The changing politics of Cuba were putting his plans to stay in serious doubt. The death of Camilo under mysterious circumstances only made it worse. Government confiscations had already begun and he felt the Finca was a prime target. His anxiety increased when René told him of an American friend who had risked his U.S. citizenship to join Fidel in the mountains in the early days of the revolution. He had been a guerrilla fighter in the U.S. Marines in the south pacific and had run guns for Castro and had been instrumental in the decisive victory at Santa Clara. Castro had rewarded him by putting him in charge of security for the Cuban air force and later made him the casino czar. But like Camilo and the others who had fought for a free Cuba, Villereal's friend had become disillusioned.

But Ernest's sleep last night had been less fitful than usual and this morning he woke up clearer. He felt like talking about the Paris book and Mary agreed. He told her he had pretty much finished it.

"What about the people you have told me about but haven't included that were good friends—will they feel left out?"

"They will be left out."

"Is there a way to list some of those and say something nice in a line or two?"

"Does it have to be something nice?"

"No."

"The notes I made in the '20s reminded me that I really didn't like some of the people who thought we were friends."

"So the Paris book is a revenge piece?"

"Wouldn't you say?"

"I haven't read it."

"But I've told you about it … I've read you parts."

"Sometimes you use names and sometimes you don't and you use a lot of nicknames that I don't recognize."

"With reason—I have means now and there are courts and people are more apt to take offense."

"So the ones you name are no longer here?"

"That could be the case."

"And the ones that are named, are remembered kindly."

"That could also be the case."

"Like Evan and Ezra and Sylvia?"

"It's difficult going in print with acid on my pen."

"Why do it then?"

"Because it's true and straight and it may explain some things to people."

"Are there others to include?"

"The notebooks are full of other people and events. I didn't miss much, sitting in the cafés. After all I was a reporter at the time and pretty much covered the who, what, where and when—this book gives the whys—and yes there are others."

"Like whom?"

"I doubt if you know them."

"I'd like to hear about them anyway—could you tell me about a few?"

He hesitated for quite a while, went to his desk and returned with a list. "Here are the ones I thought about," he said, handing it to her.

She read aloud, "Charlie Sweeney, Bill Bird, Mike Strater, Andre Masson, Jean Miro and Larry Gaines. Well I know Mike and Miro and Masson but not the other two. Why don't you tell me a little bit about them, I didn't know any of them when you did."

"If I can have a drink on the veranda."

"Okay a small one and maybe sit in the breeze by the bougainvillea."

The contract was made, the drink was made and he was going to try to recall these former friends with just some un-typed notes. A bit of a feat given his health. He knew he shouldn't have a drink, she knew he shouldn't have a drink but neither of them cared.

"It would be nice if these men were in the Paris book but it's going to have to do without them for many reasons. But I'll give you the dust jacket version.

First there's Charles Sweeney, a real brave guy who put together a squadron of volunteer American flyers who flew for the Royal Air Force. He's still around and is tall, ruddy, and kind of hawk faced with a clipped voice." He closed his eyes and squeezed his face as if trying to remember. Then he sifted through some of his notes.

"It was squadron 71 of the Royal Air Force. He had been in the French foreign Legion, the U.S. Army, the Royal Air Force and the Polish Army. A real soldier's soldier. He also fought the fascists in Spain on behalf of the Loyalists, the Bolsheviks on behalf of the Poles and the Riffs in Morocco on behalf of the French. Charlie knew how to wage war. He is also a friend of Waldo Peirce."

"Who painted your portrait," she nodded to the wall where the oil from 1929 was displayed.

"And also of Max Eastman."

"I know Max Eastman. He told me something once that made a lot of sense—it's the ability to take a joke—not make one—that proves you have a sense of humor."

She wondered if Ernest knew this was aimed in his direction.

"Well, Charlie sure was brave but he could be a pain in the neck. He was forever asking me for autographed copies of *For Whom*."

"Is he still around?"

"Yes and I still get a letter once in a while looking for an autographed book—he is still a pain in that regard but a brave pain. I always thought that wars were the best grist for a writer and certainly Sweeney had a lot of war material. War was his vocation and perhaps even his avocation but he really wasn't a player in the lost generation. All in all I decided to leave him out." He took a drink.

"Then there's Bill Bird. Bill and I go back a long way. He was the printer and editor of *The Three Mountain Press* in 1920s Paris. I knew Bill well, we spent a lot of time together talking about boxing, Ezra, Ford and Mike Strater.

"When my manuscripts had gone missing at the Gare de Lyon, Bill suggested ways I might get them back by hiring a detective, posting notices around the train station and by raising the amount of the reward. He was born in Buffalo and he wrote a book when we were in Paris in '21 or '22: *A Practical Guide to French Wine*. We all owned it and it was a handy book to have. I introduced him to Ezra, and Bill published both *In Our Time* for me and a draft of Pound's *Cantos* and *The Great American Novel* for Carlos Williams.

"Bill's a good guy and a nice man. After Paris he moved to Spain during the war, and after the war he went to Tangier. Last I heard, in a letter, he was still in Morocco. He wrote a very entertaining letter when Ezra was writing music for an opera. Bill said he was so loud, he annoyed the Swedes living above him who were never annoyed by anything."

Ernest stopped talking, tilted his head back and looked at the ceiling for a while.

"Who's next?"

"I need a minute to get organized." He took it.

"Bill Bird was also a friend of Larry Gaines who was a friend of mine. Larry was a Canadian born Negro heavyweight prizefighter who fought very well. I remember when he left Germany in the early '20s for Paris because he had beaten everyone in Germany except two fighters who refused to fight him. He had been fighting in Germany, Sweden, England and France. He had a hell of a record. He beat Max Schmeling, Primo Carnera and Jack London. I felt bad for him around that time; he was looking for a way to make himself better known stateside and he tried to train with Jack Dempsey, who would not train with a colored man.

"Gaines actually held the title, World Colored Heavyweight Champ."

"Is he still around?"

"Yes," he said amid another sip.

"And then there was Mike Strater. This is a tricky one. As you know he was Ivy League educated from a wealthy family and an expat artist that I fished and fought with. I met him at Ezra's in the early '20s but the real intrigue started in 1935 when he came to fish with me in Bimini. Two years earlier I had asked him to go to Africa with us and for reasons I never understood he refused. This angered me and I really never got over it but I invited him to Bimini in '35 because we were both really good fisherman and it was a big deal for marlins then. Mike was a hell of a fisherman and we had been friends for 13 years. We had the *Pilar* in Bimini and I shot myself in the legs trying to kill a shark but I went to a hospital and got fixed up. Nobody was catching anything until Mike hooked an honest to God 14 foot marlin that had to go 1,000 pounds or more. As I sit here in front of you, not half the man I used to be, I will tell you straight and true that I was a real son of a bitch to him on that trip. I've really never admitted that before and it's way past due. While we were all trying to land what was obviously a record catch, I did not play my part very well. In fact I screwed things up which resulted in the fish being half eaten by sharks, and I'm not sure I didn't do some of it on purpose. We managed to get it ashore without breaking its spine and there are great pictures of it hanging with Mike and me standing by. Afterwards we went to a bar and tied one on and I punched him in the gut. We had both been drinking like thirsty swordfish so I used that as an excuse but inside even then I knew it was inexcusable. So I don't have a very good feeling about Mike even though he was a very handsome, likable guy who didn't brag.

"He was a decent man who loved to fill his days with painting, shooting, fishing, boxing, hunting and reading. I think I have some of his old letters here in Cuba. He wrote great letters, long letters and funny letters. He was always positive and always stressed everyone's good points. The one I'll never forget was the one where he made fun of the cover art on the

Sun Also Rises. He said that if I thought the design was art than I was a bald assed baboon. He said it was a picture of the muse of literature just having come twice."

"Quite a description," Mary said.

"And fairly accurate."

"Since I'm closer to going out that I am coming in, I'll be honest." He stopped for a good five minutes without saying a word but just sat there staring, and then began again as if nothing had happened. The reasons I'm not including Mike are that Scott used him as Burne Halliday in *This Side of Paradise*, he turned me down for an African Safari and he caught a bigger fish than I ever did. That's a lot of truth in a short sentence and I would hope it would stay right here in this room in the Finca."

"So he will not be a part of the Paris book?"

"I don't think so."

"But he did figure in the *Old Man*?"

"When he hooked that record marlin and the sharks got it before we got it in—I knew some day I'd use that—it was too good not to."

"Was there anyone less complicated?"

"Yes I would say that Andre Masson was about as uncomplicated as a friend could be. He was a good friend of both Evan's and mine.

"He and Evan spent a lot of time worrying about each other. Actually it was heartening to see two old warriors caring about each other the way those two did. I introduced Evan to Gertrude who introduced Evan to Andre who was then a penniless young painter with promise. He had been wounded severely in the war in 1917 and was plagued by nightmares and psychological problems." Mary was sitting face-to-face with somebody who had the same symptoms. "Andre painted *The Dice Players* that we have.

"His neighbor in the early days in Paris was Miro who was somebody else I thought about including in the Paris book. The Jean Miro you know, was not the Jean Miro then."

"But that's true of all of you."

"Yes, more so with Jean. Like I said he lived next to Andre and like Masson, had psychological issues. At the time I was making the café notes, he was already famous. I remember the first letter from him was a copy of an article he cut from a French newspaper that critiqued *The Sun Also Rises*. It was just the article sans comment, it seemed to me rather cold and distant. He would also send postcards from various countries and holiday greeting cards; and it was very interesting, the more famous he became, the more he changed his signature. From a simple "Joan" written like you or I would write it, to "Miro" with an elongated M, to an M whose legs stretched three inches or more down the page. His signature was becoming part of his art and so was he. To me he always looked a little like Charles Boyer. He sent me a line once that I liked very much, he said that he tried to apply colors like words that shape poems and like notes that shape music."

"Are you not going to include Miro because he was more famous than you?"

"I guess I deserve that and that could be part of it but I think that decision would rest more on the shenanigans that I pulled with both Evan and Hadley for his painting that's in the other room."

"I don't know that story."

"I'm not sure you'd enjoy it."

"Tell me anyway," she petitioned.

"Maybe later," he said settling the matter.

"So these characters you have just described to me will not be a part of your Paris book?"

"That would be the plan."

"And I take it that all of these fellows are still alive?"

"Yes but I'm tired and I don't think I want to get into that right now."

"But as a practical matter, it would be much easier to include people who could no longer complain about anything you said. Isn't that correct?"

"I have had advice to that effect and it seems to be good advice and a matter of common sense."

"So what happens to them? At one time or another you cared for these people, do you feel any allegiance?"

"I don't think allegiance enters into it but I think I might list them in a preface or something."

"And how would you explain that?"

"I wouldn't and I don't see a need or an obligation to do so. I might just say 'for reasons of my own' or 'for understandings adequate to the author' or something like that, some of my friends are not included and it would be good if all these were in this book but for now we will have to do without them,' or something similar."

"Then they would be like removable friends?"

"Yes, after a fashion that's what they would be."

Elsewhere in his writing some hints appear for why we will have to do without them for now. A letter to Charles Fenton may hold a clue. Charles Fenton was a lot like Hemingway. He was handsome, charismatic, a good writer and affected deeply by love and war.

He suffered from depression that resulted from his experience as a Royal Air Force bomber tail gunner in 1942. He was a professor at Duke and fell in love with a graduate student causing his wife and son to leave him and make him an outcast in the closed university setting.

During a bout with despondency, like a lot of Ernest's friends, and in fact Ernest, he took his life by jumping from the roof of a hotel in Durham, North Carolina.

In a letter to Fenton, Ernest told him that he had what he called 'a wonderful novel' to write about Oak Park, Illinois but that he would never do it because he did not want to hurt living people. He was very much aware of what "living people" could do if they identified themselves in his literature.

As with the *Old Man and the Sea* there would be no need for a disclaimer about the identities of the fictional characters. The old man and the fish, as Ernest pointed out, were both dead long since and sharks would not be likely to bring libel suits. He did not wish to hurt living people or, perhaps more importantly, have them hurt him.

While writing the Paris book he chose to rough up the Fitzgeralds, Ford, Stein, Lewis and Walsh. They had all predeceased the writing of the book.

He also takes a pretty serious shot at Dos Passos who was still alive at the time but his name does not appear, rather he is referred to as the pilot fish.

He also gives shabby treatment to a deeply camouflaged "Hal," who was probably among the living as well. The six included in the preface but not included in the book were all living at the time, so at first glance it would appear that whether or not someone was deceased was paramount in the decision to include or not to include.

In a letter written but not mailed to Charles Scribner, Jr. dated April 20, 1961, Ernest warned that libel suits would follow if the book was published at that time and that Scribner's would have to bear the burden of the suits. Scribner's wanted to publish it in the fall of the year.

DENOUEMENT

Ernest was not a stranger to death. From his father's and Hadley's father's suicide, to both world wars and all those who died and took their own lives, he had seen more than his share.

Almost for good measure it seems, his mother had gifted him the .32 Smith & Wesson Civil War revolver that his father had used to kill himself. She passed it on to him like the self-destructive genes he inherited. His younger brother Leister, then 13, was in an adjacent room, heard the gunshot and found his father. Eventually he would take his own life with a borrowed handgun. He also had suffered from diabetes and depression.

Ernest's sister Ursula, granddaughter Margaux and son Gregory all died by suicide.

By 1960 Ernest's body and mind had been ravaged by a host of concussions, broken bones, diabetes, liver, kidney and spleen ruptures, paranoia and depression. At times it was as if he were merely playing at being himself. Suicide had cast its shadow on his doorstep. His body and his mind were betraying him and throughout his life he had spoken of the gift of death.

On March 29, 1959 Ernest and Mary arrived in Cuba. René, Cristobal, Mundo and the rest were there to welcome him. The house looked like a painting with the verbena, jacaranda, frangipani and bougainvillea coming into bloom. But they were only there for less than a month when, on April 22, they flew to New York where they sailed to Spain.

There they stayed with Bill Davis, the friend with a villa in Ronda. Ernest took his working Paris book with him. It was a moveable manuscript. He had done some outlining and chapter design in Spain, but he got busy when they got back to the States, in Idaho and Cuba early in 1960 where he finished his memoir.

Valerie Darby Smith, who they had met in Spain the previous year, arrived on February 8. He was 60 and she was 19—his last futile attempt at the mythical fountain. She would go on to marry his son five years later.

He wrote an article on bullfighting for *Life* magazine, then returned to Spain to finish some details while Mary stayed in Cuba. He wrote that he missed her though their marriage had waned to the point where Mary had threatened divorce.

He said he needed her to keep from cracking up. She was strong and focused and he wasn't.

Back from Spain he went to Idaho by train, Mary with him. Ernest would never leave. Arriving in Ketchum, Ernest was seriously depressed. His blood pressure was off the charts at 250/125 and he was not mentally stable.

Physically he was being defeated by his kidneys and liver which he had not treated well over the years and his diabetes was destroying him like it had destroyed his brother.

On Friday, April 21, 1960, Mary had found him sitting in the vestibule with a shotgun and two shells and a note he had written to her. She put him in the hospital in Ketchum. But death was seriously on his mind.

On Monday, April 24 Joan Higgons, his nurse at the Sun Valley Hospital, and Don Anderson, a local hunting buddy, took him home from the hospital and immediately had to wrestle a shotgun away from him and return him to the hospital. He had flirted with death since he was 19 in World War I, now he would marry her.

After his second plane crash in January 1954, he had the odd luxury of being able to read and appraise his own obituary and track how others perceived his never-ending courtship with death. All the accidents, all the wounds, all the blood—none of it could destroy him, he left that for himself.

He had abandoned Grace, his mother, and in the end he would abandon grace under pressure, that equanimity he so cherished.

On Tuesday, April 25 they flew him in a Piper Comanche to the Mayo Clinic in Rochester, Minnesota. He tried to end it twice, once by attempting to jump out mid-air and once when they stopped in Rapid City, South Dakota to refuel when he tried to walk into the propeller of another plane. He did not do well at the Mayo, especially when they administered 15 or so controversial electro shock treatments—given his history of head injuries and that a side effect of the treatments was loss of short-term memory, a critical asset to a writer.

In Cuba he had just finished his Paris book which consisted of 20 chapters of memories from 30 years ago. His memory had been stimulated by his Paris notes and now they had erased it with a bolt of lightning.

Gary Cooper, one of his true friends, who had been in Mass General for cancer treatment, died on May 13. Ernest was an honorary pallbearer.

His inability to attend only aggravated his searing sadness and profound sense of worthlessness. The next 50 days were filled with paranoia about his finances, being shadowed by the FBI and debilitating side effects of depression and agitation from long term use of his blood pressure medication.

On the early morning of July 2, he tried to end it yet again. He would have to try no more.

Sunday, July 2, 1961 he got up around 7:00 am in his home, nestled in the Sawtooth Mountains of Idaho, careful not to wake Mary. He went to a basement storeroom, picked out a favorite double-barreled 12 gauge shotgun and walked to the foyer in the front of the house. He put the cool steel of the barrels to his face, close to the bump on his forehead that he had given himself in the small loo in Paris, when by mistake he pulled a skylight window down on himself.

There would be no mistake now. He put the barrels into his mouth and reached down through all the years, through all the glories, the bullfights, the romances, the safaris, the world wars, the prizes, the marriages, the deep-sea fish. All of the adventures, and all of the sadness … he reached down through it all, pushed the trigger and followed in his father's footsteps.

Mary found him at 7:30 am and then rushed to excuse him by saying it was an accident.

Suicide had moved into his life when he was 29 and it never left. It was the ghost he couldn't kill.

Hadley, now married to Paul Mowrer, was fishing—something Ernest had taught her, when she heard. She had last written him in the spring. He had called her Cat in Paris—she had used that nickname to sign the letter.

EPILOGUE

The term moveable feast has long been part of religious nomenclature. It denotes a holy day for which the date of observance is not fixed to a date certain. A good example of a moveable feast would be Easter, which can vary by over 40 days in as much as it depends partly on the phase of the moon. As a consequence, Easter related dates are also moveable feasts.

In 1960, A.E. Hotchner was leaving the Hemingway's in Cuba to return to New York. Ernest entrusted his Paris book manuscript to him for the trip back to Scribner's. On the plane he read what he said was essentially what was eventually published. The work, however, had not been given a title. Ernest had difficulty naming it and had asked Mary for the Oxford Book of English Verse and a copy of the Bible, two sources he'd used before. Hotch supplied the title to Mary from something Ernest had said. Something to the effect that if you are lucky enough to have lived in Paris, then wherever you may go, it will stay with you, because Paris is a moveable feast.

The term can be found in other places in literature.

In 1942, in his absurdism novel, *The Stranger,* Albert Camus has one of his characters, Masson, refer to lunch as a moveable feast—one had it when one felt like it. Hemingway knew Camus and he read *The Stranger.*

From that day at the Ritz when the notebooks made a reprise, Ernest referred to his project as the Paris book. It was a traveling tale. Mary recollected that it started in Cuba in 1957 and visited Ketchum, Idaho in the winter of 1958–59, then on to Spain in April 1959 and made return trips to Cuba and Ketchum before it was finished in Cuba in the spring of 1960. From there

Hotch took it to the publisher in New York and Ernest and Mary went on their last trip to Idaho. Certainly a globetrotting composition.

The series of sketches, profiles of the literati in waiting, stars who were and were to be, is a fascinating look into the Paris of the Jazz Age, the roaring '20s. Maybe the most romantic, alluring age ever, with the most captivating and intriguing characters, told by one of the stars. It's even more compelling when we realize how compromised the author's physical and psychological health had become and how close he was to taking his life.

He is buried in Ketchum Cemetery, among the soughing pines and facing the mountains, beneath a granite slab announcing simply: Ernest Miller Hemingway, July 21, 1899–July 2, 1961.

ABOUT THE AUTHOR

Bob is a contributor to The Hemingway Review and appears in a documentary on the author. He lives with his wife in Massachusetts and Florida. They have five grown children.

Printed in Great Britain
by Amazon